SKATEBOARD
RENEGADE

The #1
Sports Series
for Kids

SKATEBOARD RENEGADE

Text by Paul Mantell

Little, Brown and Company
Boston   New York   London

To my great-granddaughter
Samantha Jo Howell

First Paperback Edition

Matt Christopher™ is a trademark of Catherine M. Christopher.

Library of Congress Cataloging-in-Publication Data

Mantell, Paul.
    Skateboard renegade / text by Paul Mantell. — 1st ed.
       p. cm.
    Summary: Wanting to fit in with his skateboarding friends, Zach is tempted to adopt a new image of spiked bleached hair and a pierced ear.
    ISBN 0-316-13487-2 (hc)/ISBN 0-316-13549-6 (pb)
    [1. Skateboarding — Fiction.   2. Identity — Fiction.]   I. Title.
PZ7.M31835 Sk   2000
[Fic] — dc21   00-035655

10 9 8 7 6 5 4 3 2 1

COM-MO

Printed in the United States of America

1

"Zachary!"

Zach Halper was in midair when he heard his mother's voice calling him. The sound threw him off, and he nearly wiped out on landing, his skateboard sliding out from underneath him.

"What do you want?" he called to her, annoyed, as he got up and dusted himself off.

"Come here, quickly!"

She sounded excited. Zach left his skateboard where it lay, on the strip of grass beside the long, wide driveway, and went inside to see what the fuss was about.

His mom was in the kitchen. She held a fat envelope in her hand and wore a big smile on her face. "It's from Amherst Academy," she announced, handing him the already-opened envelope.

Zach read it out loud. "Congratulations. You have been accepted to Amherst Academy for Technology and Computer Science...." His voice faded to a whisper. "Wow... I thought when I got put on the waiting list, that meant 'no'...."

He wasn't kidding. He really hadn't expected this. After all, it was the very end of August — only a few days till school started. He'd been on the waiting list since July 6. Now here he was, all set to go back to Brighton Middle for the start of seventh grade — back with his usual gang in the same old school — and suddenly his whole world was about to change.

"Aren't you excited?" his mom asked, still smiling broadly. "I'd have thought you'd be jumping for joy."

"Oh. Yeah, it's great!" Zach said, but a little uncertainly. Sure, he was excited — proud of himself for doing well enough on the entrance exam to get into the exclusive school. Amherst had all the most up-to-date equipment, software, and Internet connections and offered a superior program in math, science, and technology. "It's just... I'd already given up on going," he explained.

"Well, isn't this a wonderful surprise then!" his mom said, giving him a big hug and kiss. "Wait till I tell your father!" She let him go and went straight for the telephone.

It hadn't been Zach's idea to apply to Amherst Academy. His parents had practically made him do it. "You're not being challenged enough at Brighton" was what they said. "That school is going downhill fast."

Zach thought Brighton was okay. He suspected that it was his choice of friends his parents really objected to — though, of course, they always denied it.

Still, once Zach had decided to apply to Amherst — once he'd gone through the tests, the interview, and all the paperwork — he'd actually started to get excited about going. When the school had put him on the waiting list, he'd been terribly disappointed. So part of him really did feel great, now that he'd been accepted.

Zach tucked the envelope into the pocket of his shorts. He couldn't wait to tell the guys he'd made it into Amherst! He ran out the kitchen door to get his board, then stopped in his tracks. His nine-year-old sister, Zoey, was trying to ride his skateboard — and was heading right into the street!

"Hey!" he shouted at her. "Get off my board!"

She obeyed, but not on purpose. Zoey's arms flailed out to either side, and suddenly she was airborne!

The board slid out from under her and scooted into the road, where it rolled right between the front and rear wheels of a delivery truck that was barreling down the road.

Zoey sat on her butt in the driveway, sniffling back tears.

"Zoey, you idiot!" Zach scolded her. "That could have been *you* under that truck!"

"Well, if you'd given me lessons, like you promised all summer, I wouldn't stink so bad at skateboarding," she said, looking up at him accusingly.

"Aw, nuts," he said shaking his head and helping her to her feet. "I told you, I *will* . . . when I have time." He looked to make sure the coast was clear, then crossed the street and retrieved his board. It seemed none the worse for wear.

"You could at least have worn a helmet," he muttered to Zoey as he came back up the driveway.

"I was just trying to balance on it for one second," Zoey protested. "But it started rolling downhill."

"Yeah, well, one second is all it takes sometimes," Zach told her. "What if you'd landed on your head?"

"Mom would have punished *you*," Zoey said with a smug smile. "It's your skateboard, and you're supposed to be responsible for me."

"Now look," he said, shaking a finger at her, "I'm going over to Moorehead Park to see my friends. If you don't say anything about what just happened, I won't. That way, neither of us gets into trouble. Okay?"

Zoey scrunched up her face, apparently trying to figure out what kind of trouble *she* could possibly be in.

"You nearly got yourself killed by riding my board without my permission and without a helmet, okay?" Zach explained, reminding her. "So just keep quiet about it. I'll see you later."

Strapping his helmet back on and adjusting his knee, wrist, and elbow pads, he pushed off on his skateboard, rolling down the sidewalk toward Moorehead Park.

"Give my regards to your stupid friends!" Zoey called after him.

Zach smiled, not looking back. Zoey didn't like his friends, and neither did his parents. Well, too bad. They were *his* friends, not theirs.

As he went, he practiced his skateboarding skills, which were pretty good, if Zach could say so himself. He zigzagged down the gentle slope toward downtown, deftly avoiding the pedestrians he passed. He did a grab over a fire hydrant, then stopped at the traffic light at Foley and Whitmore by doing a skid stop called the cess slide.

That's the best thing about skateboarding, Zach thought as he waited for the light to change. It's so versatile. You can go places on your board or you can do tricks and perform with it. You can even slalom or go on a half pipe, just like you were on the ski slopes.

The light changed, and Zach pushed off into the road. He hopped the curb on the other side and kept on going.

Moorehead City wasn't much of a city, really. It had once been a booming mill town, and now the mills had closed. Even worse, the new mall out in

6

Oakmont had drawn shoppers away from downtown, where more and more stores these days were closing.

Still, today was the Friday before Labor Day weekend, and all the stores on Foley Square were having sidewalk sales. Zach had to skateboard out into the street to avoid all the people and tables on the sidewalk.

Right away he drew the attention of the policeman directing traffic at the corner of Foley and Main. "Hey, you! Kid! Back on the sidewalk! No skateboarding around here!" the cop yelled at him.

Zach immediately did as he was told, his face flushed with humiliation. Everyone was turning around to look at him! And what had he done that was so awful?

This town needed more places for kids to skateboard! It just wasn't fair!

Moorehead Park, on the other side of downtown, had seen better days. The rusty swings were old, and the water fountains didn't work. The whole place was due for renovation as soon as school started.

Meanwhile, the park had been pretty empty all

summer long. No mothers wanted to take their babies there. That should have made it the perfect place to go skateboarding.

Except there was one problem. The park was full of broken pavement, skateboard-stopping rubble, and broken glass! Zach had to stop, grab his board, and walk through the park entrance. You could really get cut up falling here — especially the palms of your hands. Zach wished he'd worn his skateboarding gloves instead of just wrist protectors.

He looked over to the far corner of the paved playground area. There were his friends, practicing their boarding skills on the least-broken-up section of pavement.

"Hey!" Zach called out, waving as he trotted over to join them. He stopped when he saw someone unfamiliar among the others — a kid with spiked, platinum-blond hair.

Then he realized who it was. "Jeffers? Brian, man, what did you do to your hair?"

"You like the 'do?" Brian asked with a wicked grin. "It's the new me! And hey — check this out!" He turned to show Zach that he was wearing a sparkly earring in his left ear. "I'm pierced! The first of many, man. And I'm getting a tattoo soon. The complete look, right? Ha! You should have seen my mom's face when I came home looking like this!"

"It freaked her right out," Kareem Walker said. He proudly put a hand on Brian's shoulder and, with the other hand, gave him a high five. "I was there!"

"She about fainted," Brian bragged, chuckling as he remembered the golden moment.

"We're all gonna get our hair bleached and ears pierced to match!" little Sam Vasquez announced. "Tattoos, too — right guys?"

"Right," Kareem agreed. He was tall and very dark, and was going to look awesome with bleached blond hair, Zach thought with a smile.

Sam was only starting sixth grade, but they let him hang around with them anyway. He was a pretty good boarder and a good sport, too. He let Brian tease him all day long and never stopped smiling. Besides, as Brian always pointed out when Sam wasn't around, Sam's parents owned the local sporting-goods store. It didn't hurt to be nice to their kid.

"How about you, Halper?" Brian asked him. "You gonna do it, too? We can be the Brighton Boarding Crew!"

9

The others all whooped and high-fived each other, liking the idea a lot. But Zach hesitated. He wasn't sure he wanted to bleach and spike his hair, let alone get his ear pierced. And a tattoo? Forget it!

"I don't know," Zach said. "I . . . got some news today, guys."

"What?" Farrell Simon asked, the first to pay attention.

"I got into Amherst Academy."

A sudden silence fell on the group like a shadow, darkening their expressions. Nobody said a word, or even breathed, for several seconds.

"Really?" Sam was the first to break the spell. "Wow. That's great . . . I guess."

"I thought you were only on the waiting list," Farrell said.

"I was," Zach replied. "Till today. To tell you the truth, I'd forgotten all about it myself."

"So I guess . . . you're gonna go there, huh?" Kareem said softly. "I mean, they accept you, you don't say no, right?"

"Guess not," Zach said, looking at the ground.

Only now did the horrible reality begin to sink in, and it gave Zach a sick feeling inside. They'd all be going back to Brighton Middle School in a few more days — *all except him.*

"So I guess you're not gonna get your hair bleached or any of that stuff," Farrell said sadly.

"Of course I am!" Zach insisted hotly, choking back the tears that wanted to come. *I'm still one of you guys!* he felt like telling them. But it was no good if you had to say it.

Nobody said anything for a long time.

"You know what?" Brian Jeffers broke the silence. "Moorehead Park really bites. There's nothing good to do here. Let's all go over to the school steps and ride some rails."

Zach turned to him, taken aback. "But, Brian, remember what school security said?"

"School security?" Brian repeated, as if Zach had mentioned something disgusting. "Give me a break! Hey, you're going off to nerd heaven. We've gotta give you a fitting send-off."

2

The boys boarded together to the middle school. Farrell moved up next to Zach.

"So," Farrell said, "I can't believe you're not going to be in school with us next week."

"Uh-huh," Zach said, without enthusiasm. "Neither can I."

Brian zigged up next to them. "Mr. Megabrain," Brian commented, rolling his eyes. "Pretty soon, you'll be too stuck-up to want to hang out with the likes of us."

"Shut up, Jeffers," Zach told him, forcing a laugh. "Like that would ever happen."

Inside, though, Zach wasn't the least bit amused. They'd reached the school, and Zach prayed that the conversation would end. It didn't.

"Amherst Academy — big whoop," Brian went

on. "All those weirdos, nerds, and geeks. I could never stand going to a school like that."

"You could never get *into* a school like that, dude," Farrell shot back. "You're way too dumb in math and science."

"Better than you," Brian countered.

"Yeah, right." Farrell laughed. "You're the one who thought geometry was another name for earth science, remember?"

They all laughed at that one. Looking annoyed, Brian made his way to the top landing of the school's stone steps. "Come on, you guys," he said. "Enough yammering. Let's ride some rails! Sam, you watch the sidewalk to make sure it's clear."

Sam took up his post at the bottom of the handicapped ramp, which zigzagged down the steps in four stages. The setup was perfect. You rode down the first section of ramp, then jumped the rest of the rails as you went down the sections, finally hopping off onto the sidewalk at the very bottom. It was the best place they'd ever found for ramp and rail action.

It was also against the law. A big sign on the school wall at the side of the top landing said NO EATING,

DRINKING, SPITTING, LOITERING, ELECTIONEERING, SOLICITING, OR SKATEBOARDING!

Which was why Zach had had his doubts about coming. *Oh, well,* he thought with a sigh. *It's probably okay, just for a little while — just this once.*

First one down was Farrell Simon, tall and athletic, and the best ramp rider among them. Bending down to grab his board as he sailed down the first ramp, he let out a whoop and leaped onto the handrail. He rode it down, straddling it with his rail bar, then went airborne at the bottom.

"Way to go, Farrell!" Zach yelled as his friend hit the pavement and rolled off in a lazy circle, his fists raised over his head in triumph. The rest of them cheered, too — except for Brian Jeffers.

Brian had a way of being sarcastic and doing the opposite of what everybody else did. He'd throw you a compliment, only it sounded like an insult. Zach didn't think much of Brian's sense of humor, but since everyone else always seemed to find Brian funny, he laughed along with the rest.

"Simon, you call that rail riding? You stink!" Brian called out, slapping his knee like he'd said something hilarious. Sure enough, the others all laughed and clapped their hands on cue.

Jerry Sinclair was next up, but he wasn't all that good a boarder, so he started from the second landing, halfway down the steps. From that height, riding only the bottom rail, a fall wouldn't break too many bones.

"All clear!" Sam shouted, and Jerry pushed off.

"What a wuss!" Brian shouted as Jerry failed to make the railing on his first try, and wound up doing a somersault on the sidewalk to keep from hurting himself. "Next!"

That meant it was Kareem's turn. "S-somebody else go," he stammered. "I've got a foot cramp." He bent over as if in pain, but Zach could tell he was faking it.

Kareem wasn't wearing a helmet or any safety gear — he could be a real big shot when they were just hanging around the playground, practicing wheelies, ollie flips, and kick turns. But it was another thing when you were doing really dangerous stunts like this.

"What are you, chicken?" Brian razzed him. "Look,

15

man, there's nothing to it." Brian wasn't wearing a helmet, either. He never did. Unlike Kareem, though, Brian didn't seem to care about the danger. Without an "all-clear" from Sam down below, he pushed off from the top landing, riding the rails all the way down to the street.

Brian was good, and Zach and the others got caught up in watching his ride. It was only at the last moment, when Brian was about to leap off the bottom rail for his landing, that they heard Sam's warning cry, followed by a woman's scream.

She was coming down the sidewalk, pushing a baby stroller. Brian, airborne, barreled straight into her. The woman screamed as she toppled over backward. She let go of the stroller, and it rolled quickly toward the curb, beyond which cars were racing down the boulevard.

Zach and the others cried out in horror. Luckily, Farrell, who was already on the sidewalk, ran over and grabbed the stroller just in time. The baby inside started hollering at the top of its lungs.

"My baby!" the woman screamed. "What happened to my baby?"

"The baby's okay, ma'am," Farrell assured her, walking the stroller back over to her. Brian was trying to help the woman up, but she yanked her arm free.

"Don't touch me or my baby!" she shouted, grabbing the stroller away from Farrell. "Help!" she yelled, looking around in panic. "Somebody help me! My baby! My baby!"

Whether it was just bad luck or a twist of cruel fate, at that very moment a police car came around the corner. It pulled over with a screech of brakes, and Sergeant Raphael Rizzo got out. Zach knew Sargeant Rizzo from school, where he gave D.A.R.E. lectures.

Rizzo knew all of *them*, too. "These kids botherin' you, Mrs. Bailey?" he asked the woman.

"They certainly are, Officer," Mrs. Bailey told him. "That one knocked me down. My baby was almost killed!"

Rizzo turned to Brian. "And what do you have to say for yourself, Blondie?" he asked Brian.

"I didn't see her!" Brian said, his voice cracking with fear. No more sarcasm now, Zach noticed.

Brian looked from one of his friends to another. "Sam, you were supposed to warn us if anyone was coming!" he said.

Sam's lower lip quivered. "How'd I know you were gonna take off like that? You didn't warn *me!*" he protested. "I turned around, and you were already halfway down!"

"All right — every last one of you, get in the car," Sergeant Rizzo ordered. "I'll take it from here, Mrs. Bailey. You sure you're all right now?"

"Yes, thank you, Officer," Mrs. Bailey said.

"And the baby?"

"She'll be all right."

"Well, then." He tipped his cap to her and went around to the driver's side.

Squashed inside the squad car, the boys shot one another furtive looks. "Oh, man!" Kareem whispered, his eyes panicked. "What are we gonna do now?"

"You think they'll put us in jail?" Jerry wondered.

"I told you guys last time we weren't allowed to skateboard here!" Sam said. "But nobody listens to me."

Brian gave Sam a sharp elbow. "Shut up, you

twerp," he muttered as Sergeant Rizzo got in and started the car.

Zach sat silently in the backseat, crammed in among the rest of them, wondering what was going to happen next. He'd never been in trouble before — nothing this big, anyway. He'd always gotten decent grades and had a good reputation. Until now.

Sure, he always hung out with Brian and Jerry and the others. And once in a while they got chased by an angry storeowner who didn't want them boarding in front of his store or in his parking lot. But none of the boys had ever seen the inside of a police car before!

It had all happened so quickly, too. One minute they were hanging out, fooling around, having some fun. The next minute they were a bunch of juvenile delinquents, on their way to a life behind bars!

"Now, haven't I told you boys a million times those steps are off-limits?" Sergeant Rizzo said. "I nailed that sign up myself, but does it do any good? No! I feel like I've been talking to a wall, you know?" They watched the back of his head shaking back and forth with disappointment. None of them said a word.

"That little baby could have been killed," Rizzo went on. "And that lady could have been seriously hurt. Those skateboards of yours are dangerous. Don't you kids get it?" He shook his head again. "They oughta take those things away from you . . . make you do some homework for a change."

"It was just an accident," Brian pointed out.

"And it's not like we have anyplace safe to go," Farrell said.

"And what about Moorehead Park?" the sergeant asked, driving in traffic now.

"Yeah, right," Brian muttered. "Maybe after they repave it, and if they cleaned up the broken glass once in a while. Man, we are so persecuted in this town! Wherever we go, we get chased. And all we're trying to do is have some fun."

"You call those things fun?" the policeman asked, snorting in utter disgust. "Gee whiz! You kids kill me. Especially you two, without the helmets even!" He turned onto a side street and pulled the squad car over.

"Hey," Jerry said suddenly, his voiced choked with fear. "This is *my* street."

"That's right." Rizzo said, nodding his head now.

"But I thought you were taking us down to the station," Jerry said nervously.

"Nope. I'm gonna drop you kids off one by one, and see what your parents have to say about this."

A chill went up and down Zach's spine. He looked around at his friends and saw that they were panicking, too.

Telling their parents? That was much worse than going to jail!

Zach and the others watched from the backseat of the squad car as Jerry Sinclair's mother yelled at him. Then she grabbed his ear and pulled her son inside, slamming the door behind them.

Oh, boy, Zach thought. *This is not looking good.*

One by one, the other kids were dropped off. Zach watched them all go, looking as though they were on their way to the electric chair. He could only imagine what his parents were going to say when they saw him come home in a police car!

3

It was even worse than he could have imagined. There was no yelling, like at some of the other kids' houses. Instead, and far worse, he got the disappointed looks, the shaking heads, the tears in his mother's eyes — and last but not least, the lecture.

"Skateboards are dangerous things," his dad began. "We thought you were mature enough to handle the responsibilities."

"I am, Dad," Zach replied lamely. "It wasn't my fault. . . ."

"This is not about blame," said his mother.

But Zach knew that it was. He was to blame for letting his parents down. They were to blame for not raising him better. He ran up to his bedroom and shut the door behind him.

Their voices followed him:

"There'll be no more skateboarding before school starts!" his dad said, sounding angry.

"And you're to stay around the house, where we can keep an eye on you, do you hear?" his mom added.

Zach heard them all right, but he didn't say anything. He waited until their voices faded down to a murmur. Then he slowly, silently opened his door and crept halfway back down the stairs, to hear what they were saying to each other in private — the real deal, not the stupid lecture stuff they gave him, as though he were a three-year-old or something!

"I'm *so* glad he got into Amherst," Zach heard his mom say.

"Yeah," his dad agreed. "He wasn't going to learn anything good from those kids at Brighton. Maybe he'll fall in with a better class of kid at Amherst."

A better class of kid? Zach could feel the blood pounding in his ears. He had to bite down on his lower lip to keep from screaming down at them.

"Those are my friends you're talking about!" he would have said. "I picked them, and I like them, and they like me, and it's none of your business who I hang out with!"

But he just sat there, listening to see if they would say anything else outrageous.

"He's such a bright boy," his mom went on. "He should be hanging around with gifted children."

"Some of those Brighton kids have been in trouble before," his dad interjected. "I heard someone say Jerry Sinclair got caught shoplifting last year."

Yeah. A piece of gum. Zach shook his head in despair. Jerry had only done it on a dare from Brian Jeffers, who would never have tried to do such a thing himself. Okay, so Jerry had made a mistake, and like a moron, he'd gotten himself caught by a policeman who'd come into the store to buy some breath mints. Caught red-handed.

Jerry was now a two-time loser. No wonder his mom had grabbed him by the ear like that. She'd probably chew it right off for him. But one thing she wouldn't do — she wouldn't send Jerry to another school, just to keep him away from his friends!

Though Zach normally got along with his mom and dad, at moments like this he really hated them. Why were they punishing him? Because Brian hadn't warned Sam to be on the lookout? Because Zach had followed Brian and the others to Brighton Middle so they wouldn't have to skateboard over broken glass?

And wasn't sending him to Amherst punishment enough? Why did they have to ground him for the next three days — his last three days before school started? These might be the last days he ever got to hang out with his old friends!

Zach crept back up the stairs. On the way to his bedroom, he passed the open door of his sister's room. Zoey, nine years old, had become a real pain lately, always wanting Zach's attention. She was in her room now, playing with her little friend Lorena.

"Hi, Thack," Lorena said. She had a really thick lisp. Zach sometimes felt like imitating it, but he never did. Lorena worshiped Zach, and he knew it would have hurt her feelings if he'd made fun of her. But he was sure there were lots of others kids who did.

"Hi, Lorena," he said. "Hey, Zoey."

"You got in trouble," Zoey said, smiling wickedly.

"No duh!" Zach replied. "You are so smart, Zoey. How did you figure that out? Was it the policeman?"

Zoey giggled, and so did Lorena. "Are you going to jail, Thack?" Lorena asked.

Zach thought of Amherst Academy. It didn't have bars on the windows, but if he didn't have any friends there, it was going to feel like jail all right.

"Thoey theth you promithed to give her thkate-boarding lethonth," Lorena said.

"I did," Zach told her. "I will, okay? Soon."

"When?" Zoey asked.

"I don't know! Soon! Now leave me alone!"

Zach went into his room and shut the door behind him to get away from those two little pests. He sat on his bed, bitter but determined. He would show his parents they couldn't push him around and tell him what to do. He would be friends with whom-ever he wanted!

"Yo, Zach!"

Through his window, he could hear Jerry's harsh whisper coming from the driveway below.

Zach got off the bed and looked down. It was after dark now, but by the light of the porch lamp, Zach could see that Jerry was on his bike, not his board. He waved at Zach, motioning for him to come down and talk.

Zach went down the stairs quietly. His dad was watching the ballgame intently. From the sound of the stadium crowd, it seemed like something exciting was happening. Good. Zach got past his dad easily, without his even noticing, and slipped out the side door to the driveway.

"Guess what? Brian's dad let him have it with the belt!" Jerry told him.

"Shhh! Not so loud. How's your ear?" Zach asked.

"Sore," Jerry admitted. "What'd you get?"

"Just a lecture," Zach said. "And a grounding. I can't go boarding between now and when school starts."

"That bites," Jerry said. "Listen — we're all going tomorrow to get our ears pierced and our hair bleached. Wanna come?"

"If I'm allowed," Zach said. And then he thought, *Wait a minute! "If I'm allowed?"*

"Oh, what the hey? I'm there, no matter what!" he told Jerry. The boys exchanged an elaborate handshake, and Jerry took off on his bike.

"There," Zach said under his breath. He would spend his last days of freedom any way he felt like it! He would get his hair bleached like the rest of his friends! And he'd get his ear pierced, too! Hey — maybe he'd even get a tattoo!

4

Back in his room, Zach checked his wallet and his money box. He'd done some baby-sitting over the summer, for kids whose parents both worked. He'd even sat for Lorena once or twice, even though it meant putting up with Zoey, too.

With all his trips to the mall and to the movies with his buddies, Zach knew that it had been an expensive summer and that he'd spent most of his earnings. Still, there had to be *something* left over.

He counted out sixteen measly dollars. Where had all the rest of it gone?

He thought back. Candy binges, souvenirs when the family went on vacation, and those cool shades he'd bought himself . . . boy, the money sure went fast, now that he was earning his own!

Well, he could probably get his ear pierced for

that amount. *Or* he could get a regular haircut, without the bleaching or spiking. But no way was sixteen dollars enough for both!

Zach had no idea how much it would cost to make his hair look like Brian's, but it had to be more than a regular haircut. That amount, plus the piercing?

He needed to borrow some bucks so he could stay down with his crew. He didn't think there was any chance of getting a loan from his parents, let alone of their paying for his "new look." Not after the little incident with the policeman.

Of course, there was always Zoey — more to the point, there was Zoey's big pink piggy bank!

A brilliant plan formed in Zach's mind in an instant. He would borrow the money from Zoey's bank, then earn it back baby-sitting and return the money before Zoey ever got wise!

He stared out his door, across the hall, and through the open door of Zoey's room. There was the piggy bank tempting him on top of her bureau.

Where had Zoey and Lorena gone anyway? Zach looked out the window. There they were, in the backyard.

Good, he thought. At least she wasn't riding his board anymore.

"I'll pay her back before she even knows the money's gone," Zach assured himself as he went into Zoey's room and picked up her piggy. Turning it over, he opened the plastic twist bottom and took out the bills and change.

His sister had saved for this money over the course of who knew how long. It looked to Zach as though she'd never spent a dime of it on anything.

"Unbelievable," Zach said. "There has to be fifty dollars here at least!" He counted out forty in bills, then put the rest back in the piggy. The coins would make a nice *ka-ching* if for some bizarre reason Zoey happened to get suspicious and shake her piggy to make sure her money was still there.

Zach figured he could make up the forty bucks — if he even spent it all — in a couple of nights of baby-sitting. Feeling satisfied with himself, he screwed the plastic piece on again and replaced the piggy on the bureau. He tiptoed back to his room, the bills snug in his pocket.

Fifty-six bucks ought to be enough, he figured. Man, he couldn't wait to see his parents' faces when he came home looking like a whole new person!

Zach's parents put up a fuss when he said he wanted to go to the mall, but when he told them he needed a haircut, they took one look at his hair and agreed. It had gotten long and unruly over the summer, and he really did need a cut, any way you looked at it.

Besides, he'd just spent fifteen minutes messing it up as badly as he could.

His mom insisted on driving him, just to make sure he didn't have the pleasure of using his skateboard. Zach got out at the mall and said, "You don't have to pick me up. I'll get a lift home with one of the other kids' parents."

"What if you can't?" his mom asked.

"Then I'll walk."

"Walk? It's two miles!"

"It'll be good for me," he said, an edge of sarcasm in his voice. "I need the exercise, *since I'm not allowed to go skateboarding.*"

His mom glared at him. "Wiseguy," she muttered.

"All right. Walk home." As she drove off, he heard her mutter, "I can't wait till the school year starts."

Zach's first stop was Hair Apparent, where he asked how much it would be to have his hair bleached and done in spikes.

"For you, cutie? I'll knock five bucks off the price," the stylist on duty told him. She had two rings in each ear, one in each nostril, and one in her tongue. She looked about seventeen years old.

Zach found himself staring at the rings. *Man,* he thought, *it must have hurt to get pierced all those times!* The idea of doing it even once was already giving him the shivers.

"You like 'em?" she asked, guessing what he was looking at.

"Um, yeah," he said, embarrassed that he'd been caught. "Did it . . . I mean, did it —"

"Did it hurt? You *bet* it did," she said with a smile. "Thinking of getting pierced yourself?"

"Uh-huh."

"I recommend Hot-Cha, down at the other end of the mall. They give you a free earring with each piercing."

Hey, that was probably how Brian Jeffers had got his diamond stud earring. It was probably fake and came with the piercing. That had to be it — nobody would have bought Brian a diamond, and he sure didn't have the money to buy one himself.

"Cool," Zach said, fighting down the feeling of panic that was slowly rising inside him. "Um, how much is it?"

She quoted him a price.

"Thanks," Zach said. He did some quick mental arithmetic. He figured he had just enough money for everything, even including sales tax.

Zach felt his knees go weak. Was he really going to go through with this? He needed time to think.

Where are the guys? he wondered. Maybe he'd wait till they arrived, and they'd all do it together. Jerry hadn't said what time they were coming. Zach sure hoped they hadn't already been and gone.

"You wanna get bleached or not?" the girl asked as he turned to go.

"In a while."

"I've got an opening now. Later, you might have to wait."

"Oh." Zach hesitated. "I'm kind of waiting for

33

some friends of mine. We're all gonna get it done together," he explained to the stylist.

"Oh, honey, I've already done three or four of these cuts today. Some boys were in here earlier — it's a very popular style right now."

"Oh. That must have been them." Zach said, recovering some of his courage. "In that case, let's do it."

Forty-five minutes later he looked at himself in the mirror and nearly screamed out loud. He looked *awful!*

No, wait a minute, he told himself. *It's just the shock of seeing myself like this. It really looks okay. I mean, it's not that bad — I think.*

"How do you like it?" the girl asked.

"Awesome," he lied. He *hated* it.

"Okay, then, that'll be thirty-eight, including tax," she said, taking the towel off him and shaking it out.

Zach fished for the bills he'd stuffed in his pockets. He wondered if there was any way to put his hair back the way it had been before. But of course, even if there was a way, he couldn't afford it anymore.

"Here you go," he said, giving the stylist a two-dollar tip, just to show her he was pleased with the haircut.

"Gee, thanks!" she chirped happily. "Enjoy!"

Zach gave her a little wave as he turned in the direction of Hot-Cha. As he walked through the mall, he suddenly felt sick to his stomach.

"You're my twenty-fourth piercing today, so don't worry about a thing," the bearded man at Hot-Cha told Zach. "It only hurts for a year or so. Ha-ha! Just kidding." He laughed long and hard as he sterilized his instrument.

The blood was pounding in Zach's ears. He wondered if it would come spurting out when the guy stuck him. *Hey, what if they can't stop the bleeding?* he wondered.

"Did a bunch of kids with hair like mine come in here before?" he asked, his voice quivering a little.

"Not that I can remember," the guy said with a crooked-tooth smile. "There were a bunch of guys in here before, but I don't remember them having hair like yours."

Zach shrugged. Okay, maybe they'd come in here first, and *then* gotten their hair done. He'd probably just missed them.

"I can't remember much anymore," the bearded man was saying. "Not since my second breakdown. Ha-ha!" When Zach didn't laugh along with him, the man said, "Don't get nervous, kid — I'm just tryin' to loosen you up, get you laughing a little."

"Oh. Ha! Yeah," Zach said, trying his best. "Should I close my eyes? I guess I should close my eyes."

"Honest, this'll only hurt for a minute."

"Am I gonna bleed?"

"Just a little."

"Oww!"

"There. See? Beautiful. I never miss." The guy put down the instrument, which was kind of like a hole puncher for putting holes in paper. He took a little steel bolt and fastened it into Zach's ear. "It'll keep the hole open while it heals," he explained, dabbing it with a disinfectant that made Zach wince.

"Don't you have a little diamond stud or something?" Zach asked hopefully.

"I've got 'em for sixty-five dollars," the man said.

"Sixty-five dollars?!"

"Oh, you probably want one of the cut-glass kind. I'm all out of those. Sorry."

Great. Just great.

"Have a look at yourself, kid." The man turned Zach's chair to face the mirror.

Zach contemplated himself. Okay, he looked like a freak — but at least the hair looked a little better with the earring to match. All he needed now was a tattoo to complete the whole image.

The trouble was, Zach still didn't *feel* like the guy in the mirror. It was more like putting on a Halloween costume or something. Like a disguise.

"Man, I've still gotta get used to it," he told the bearded guy.

"It takes a while," the man agreed, nodding wisely and taking Zach's last fifteen dollars. "See you next time."

"Sure," Zach said with a little wave. Under his breath, he muttered. "Not if I see you first."

He came out of the shop and checked himself out in the mirrored pillars that flanked the mall's promenade. Yeah, the look was startling, all right. Spiky blond hair, big metal bolt in his ear, the new pair of wide-leg skateboard jeans his parents had bought him last month, and his huge designer T-shirt. All he needed to top if off was one of those tattoos Brian said he was going to get.

"Ha! Yeah, that'll be the day. He'd never go that far. . . ." Suddenly, a horrifying possibility entered Zach's mind — what if he did? The thought of getting all the needles it took for a tattoo made Zach get goose bumps all over. He hated needles worse than anything!

Zach headed for the mall exit. He guessed he'd missed his buddies, but he didn't mind walking home alone. It would give him a chance to check out the reactions of the people he passed on the street.

He took one last look at himself in the mall's plate-glass windows. Overall, he thought he looked pretty silly. The one thing he kind of liked was the earring — and even that should have been a diamond, not a steel bolt. The bolt was just for widening the hole. It didn't really look like jewelry.

Oh, well, it was too late to turn back now. And at least he'd be down with his friends.

"Besides," he told himself, "it'll all be worth it, just to see the looks on Mom and Dad's faces!"

5

His mother and father did not give Zach the exaggerated reaction he was hoping for. His mom raised one eyebrow and said, "Well, well." His dad just shook his head in disgust, muttering something Zach couldn't make out.

"You like it?" Zach asked, taunting them to tease a reaction out of them. For once in his life, he actually *wanted* to get yelled at, and they wouldn't even give him the satisfaction of acting annoyed!

"It's not important whether your father and I like it," his mother said calmly. "It's whether *you're* happy with it. You're the one who's going to have to show up at Amherst Academy looking like that."

"Like *what?*" Zach demanded.

"Zachary," his father warned. "Don't push it."

"Why don't you tell me I have to get rid of it?" Zach asked, half hoping they would.

"Of what? The hairdo?" his father said. "Oh, no. You chose it, now you can live with it. It doesn't bother us one bit."

"Not one bit," his mom echoed.

Cheese whiz! Zach thought, sighing. *Thanks a lot!* He turned and went upstairs, shaking his head.

As he got to the top step, Zoey came out of her room. Seeing him, she let out a scream worthy of a grade-B horror movie. Then she backed into her room, slamming the door behind her.

Zach heard the lock turn in the latch. "Zoey, it's me!" he called to her. "Open up!"

"Z-Zach?" He heard her quaking voice from behind the door.

"Yeah. Come on now, it's not that bad!"

She flipped the lock and slowly opened the door — just a crack, so she could peek through at him. She quickly let out a terrified squeak and shut it again.

"Zoey!"

"Okay, okay." She opened the door, wider this time. After looking at him soberly for about five seconds, she suddenly burst out laughing. "Zach, what did you do to yourself, you dummy?" she asked. "Omigosh! You look so gross!"

"I do not! Shut up!" Zach shot back, feeling the sting of tears come to his eyes. Not wanting to let her see him cry, he stormed into his room and slammed the door behind him.

No sooner had he collected himself than Zoey came in. Her face had changed now, from amused to angry. "Hey!" she said, narrowing her eyes at him. "Where'd you get the money to do all that stuff to yourself? And don't tell me mom and dad gave it to you, either!"

"I, um, I had some baby-sitting money left over . . . ," Zach fumbled.

"Yeah, right," Zoey said. "You never saw a dime you didn't spend." And then something dawned on her. "My piggy!" she cried. Wheeling around, she sped back across the hall into her room.

"Zoey, wait — !" he called after her, and sprang off the bed, hoping to prevent total disaster.

She was shaking the piggy when he came into her room. Hearing the coins inside, she began to calm down.

"You see?" he told her. "It's all still there. I told you."

She stopped shaking the pig, and stared right at him. "Oh yeah? That's what you say. But I've known you too long, you sneak!" She twisted open the bottom of the bank and quickly counted the money, her jaw hardening. "Aha!" she cried in furious triumph. "There's forty dollars missing. You thief! I'm telling!"

"No! Wait!" he ordered in a hoarse whisper. "Don't tell. I only borrowed it — I was going to pay it right back!"

"Sure you were."

"I was! With interest!"

"You must think I'm stupid," Zoey told him.

Man, she always saw right through him! "Okay, okay, don't believe me," Zach said miserably, plopping down on her bed. "Go ahead, tell them. My life's already a total wreck. You might as well light the match and set the whole thing on fire." He was surprised to find himself crying real tears, right in front of her.

The sight of him blubbering like that must have really shaken Zoey up, because she just stood there.

Her mouth was wide open, ready to call in their parents — but she kept silent, stunned by his out-pouring.

"Go ahead," Zach continued through stifled sobs. "I deserve it."

"Well," Zoey said, "maybe you could make it up to me."

Zach sniffed. "How?" he asked, totally humbled.

"You know what I really want." Zoey was staring at him.

"You mean . . . ?"

"I want skateboarding lessons," she said. "For me *and* Lorena. A *lot* of lessons. And they'd better be good."

"How many lessons?" Zach asked.

"Let's see . . . I think I'm entitled to, oh, say, two lessons a week for two months. Starting tomorrow."

"What?!"

"Take it or leave it." She crossed her arms and waited for him to decide.

Zach smiled through his tears and put a hand softly on Zoey's shoulders. "You drive a hard bar-gain, kid," he told her.

Zoey smiled, satisfied, and Zach grinned back. All in all, considering what had happened, he thought he'd gotten off pretty easy.

Sure, he'd be beholden to Zoey and her friend Lorena for the next two months — but things would have been a lot worse if she'd told their parents. He was already a disobedient troublemaker and a liar in their eyes — all he needed was for them to find out he was a thief!

Zach finally got the reaction he wanted on Labor Day, when the whole family went to visit Grandma and Grandpa Halper and all the Halper cousins. The adults groaned and moaned, and gave him lectures about his future and about being a sheep blindly following the herd and about the evils of "pop culture."

"He's gonna be just like Seymour," Aunt Belle said, shaking her head and clucking her tongue.

"You mean, 'Skeeter'?" Uncle Fred asked sarcastically. "That's what he calls himself these days, you know — what kind of a name is that, 'Skeeter'? It's short for *mosquito,* isn't it?"

Zach loved his uncle Skeeter, his mom's younger

brother. "The retro-hippie," she sometimes called him, but she always smiled when she talked about him. And every week they talked for a long time on the phone.

"Mosquito? Why would he name himself after a mosquito?" Aunt Belle wondered.

"What can I tell you?" Uncle Fred said with a shrug. "He lives out there in Los Angeles someplace and never gets a job. I don't know how he lives."

"Anyway," Aunt Belle said with another look at Zach, "this one takes after him."

Zach remembered the time Uncle Skeeter came to stay with them for a week, when Zach was only five. Skeeter hadn't been too grown up to play with him. It was like being with a very big kid, Zach remembered. Hey, if he reminded them of Uncle Skeeter, that was okay with him.

Zach tried to ignore their muttering and the looks they were giving him. Taking a hint from Uncle Skeeter, he concentrated his attention on the little kid cousins, who obviously thought Zach was the coolest thing on wheels.

"How do you make your hair stick up like that?" little cousin Marcella wondered.

"Did it hurt when they stuck a hole in your ear?" cousin Nicky asked. "I'd be too chicken to let anyone do that to me."

"You're so brave!" Marcella said, gazing at him with open admiration.

Well, it *had* taken guts to do what he'd done, Zach thought proudly. He'd gone in alone, too, without his friends there to support him.

Yeah, brave, that's me, he thought, almost believing it.

The next morning he was still thinking about his heroics as he stood in front of the bedroom mirror, getting ready for his first day at Amherst Academy.

Zach still thought the haircut looked ridiculous on him. But the stylist had assured him it was way cool, and the little kids all liked it — except for Zoey, who didn't count — so he guessed it looked okay after all.

All in all, Zach was feeling pretty good about things, considering that he was going to a new school, where everyone else knew one another, and he didn't know one single solitary soul.

Gazing at himself in the mirror, he held his hands

46

out to either side, pretending he was skateboarding. Today, with his grounding over, he'd go right over to Moorehead Park after school to see the guys. They'd compare haircuts and earrings and first days of school. He wanted to let them know he was still one of them, even if he did go to a different school now.

Zach struck another pose — as if he'd just pulled off an amazing stunt on his board and was basking in the applause of the crowd. That's when he heard Zoey laughing and clapping behind him.

"Whoo-oo!!" she catcalled, mocking him by striking a pose herself. "There he is, Mr. Cool himself!"

Zach was about to say something nasty. But then he thought, *No, I'm the mature one. I'll just let it go by, like it doesn't bother me.* And he did, chillin' as he walked past her toward the front door. "Yeah, that's right," he said. "I *am* Mr. Cool."

"Let's go, you two. Mom and I have to get to work!" Dad called from the car.

Zoey got dropped off first. She still went to good old Coleridge Elementary. Zach shook his head as he watched her walk up the steps with her little girl-friends. *Zoey doesn't know how lucky she is,* he thought. Zach still had great memories from his years at Coleridge.

He wondered if Amherst would be any better than Brighton. Everyone always said it was a better school. And when he let himself think about it, Zach was kind of excited about working on the high-tech, cutting-edge equipment Amherst offered.

But his parents hadn't sent him to Amherst for the education. No, they'd sent him there to separate him from his best friends in the world! They didn't deserve the satisfaction of seeing him get excited about it.

He got out at curbside in front of the school, and his parents called, "Good luck!" Zach ignored them. Hitching up his backpack, he turned away from the car and didn't look back as it drove off.

The first thing he noticed about Amherst Academy was that nobody, not one person, looked anything like he did.

He searched everywhere in the crowd of students milling around in front of the school. Most were dressed preppy style. Obviously, some kids still let their parents choose their clothes. "A lot of geeks and no freaks," Zach muttered to himself unhappily.

The next thing he noticed was that he was drawing stares from some of the kids. They were looking at him with a mix of curiosity, amusement, and disgust — as though he were some weird new insect who was going to be sharing a classroom with them.

Great. This was going to be just great.

Zach decided that the best thing to do was ignore them. He went up the steps and into the main hallway, where a big sign said PLEASE TAKE A SEAT IN THE AUDITORIUM.

Zach sat in the back row, where he got a good view of the rest of the student body as they filed in. He hadn't realized just how much of an outsider his "new look" would make him here. He'd done everything to fit in with his *old* friends. But he didn't go to school with them anymore. These kids were the ones he was going to have to fit in with from now on. And he looked all wrong!

The auditorium was filling up fast, and the seats around Zach were soon occupied. On his left was a fat kid with thick black glasses and braces. *Boy*, thought Zach. *Three strikes against him. Poor guy.*

"Hi!" the kid said in a squeaky voice, giving Zach

a smile full of metal. "I'm Benny Santangelo. Seven-four." He stuck his hand out, and Zach took it.

"Zach Halper. What do you mean, seven-four?" The kid looked to be about five foot two.

"My class," Benny explained. "What's yours?"

"Oh. I don't even know," Zach replied. "Let's see here . . ." He fished out his program card. Benny took it and looked it over.

"Lucky us!" he said, pointing to a number at the top right of the card. "We're classmates!"

"Great," Zach said, trying to force a smile. He was sure the kid was going to want to sit next to him, and eat lunch with him, and be his new best friend. Heelllppp!!!

The kid to the right of Zach said hello to Benny. "This is Zach," Benny told him. "I forget your last name."

"Halper," Zach said.

"Hi. I'm Bernard." The kid stuck out his hand for Zach to shake. It felt like a cold, dead fish.

Bernard was about a foot taller than Benny, but they both had exactly the same glasses. The piece of tape was even in the same spot — although Benny had actually used a Band-Aid on his.

"Pleased to meet you," Zach mumbled, then swung around to look elsewhere.

Bernard, seeing that Zach was ignoring him, started talking to Benny. Zach listened to them jabber about the fact that they were both taking Algebra 1A and Geophysical Science. Benny told Bernard he'd lost ten pounds over the summer, and Bernard said he'd grown six inches. The two boys made a date to play chess after school.

Zach sat there, rolling his eyes.

Brian Jeffers was right, he thought. *This place is nerd heaven!*

6

Zach trudged through his first classes like a robot. He said hi to the few kids who said hi to him. The others he ignored. He could hear them whispering behind his back. Zach was feeling worse than ever about his new look — the hair, the stupid bolt in his ear, and especially his wide-leg skater jeans.

These kids have probably never been on a skateboard in their lives, he decided. Amherst didn't have much of a sports program.

But, boy, were the kids here ever smart! Zach really had to listen hard to keep up with what was being taught, even on the first day of classes. He could see this wasn't going to be a free ride to the honor roll, like at Brighton last year. Amherst was a very serious place.

He struggled through the morning — math, science, and Spanish — and made his way to the cafeteria for lunch.

Things began to look up the minute he smelled the food. *Real* food! Not school cafeteria variety: two weeks old, overcooked, and underseasoned. Zach got himself some yummy-looking lasagna, fresh salad, and a side of cooked apples.

He scanned the big room for a free seat next to a friendly face. But the only face he recognized was Benny's.

"Have a chair," Benny said, motioning for Zach to sit down. "How's it going so far? Not so good, huh?"

Zach was taken aback. "Is it that obvious?" he asked.

Benny shrugged. "First day in a new environment. Plus you look different than everybody else, which makes it worse. Believe me, I know."

"Oh." Zach nodded, looking at Benny. "I see what you mean."

"I've always been big," Benny confided. "Something in my genes, you know? I really don't eat much — plus I'm a vegetarian. No cheese, no nothing. Did you ever meet a fat vegetarian before?"

Zach laughed. "Nope, can't say that I have."

"Well, you just met your first," Benny said. "Probably your last, too. Oh, well. Everybody gets bad breaks. Gotta live with 'em. So what's yours?"

Zach smiled. "I went and got this done to myself over the weekend," he confessed. "Isn't that stupid?"

"Thought you'd fit in better?" Benny asked dryly. "Good call. You blend in really well — with the food, of course. Not the kids."

Hey, Zach thought, cracking up. *This kid is really funny!*

"Amherst is okay," Benny told him between bites of his food. "It's hard, but the teachers are good, and most of them are pretty fair. Anyway, it's way better than my old school, Kingsway. I used to get tortured there every single day. Kids will look at you funny here, but they won't flush your head in the toilet or pull on your underwear or anything."

Zach's eyes widened. "That actually happened to you?" he gasped. Benny only shrugged, but Zach could see the pain in his eyes. *Poor kid,* he thought. *He really needs a friend here — and so do I.*

"My friends from Brighton all got their hair bleached and their ears pierced," Zach explained.

54

"Oh, I see," said Benny. "You're in a gang?"

"No, not really," Zach said with a chuckle. "We all skateboard, so we're kind of a crew, I guess. We did get in trouble with the police last week, for boarding on the steps at Brighton School."

"Wow!" Benny said, impressed. "You're a bad dude, huh?"

"Yeah, that's me," Zach said, cracking up again. "You're pretty funny, you know that?"

"So I'm told," Benny said. "It helps to have a sense of humor, 'specially if you're me." Finished with his food, Benny picked up his tray. "I've gotta go. I've got Software Design next period."

"Hey, me too!" Zach said. "I'll come with you."

"Listen, what club are you gonna join?" Benny asked as they walked.

"I don't know," Zach said. He remembered the principal talking about clubs during the assembly, but Zach hadn't really been paying attention. He'd been too busy checking out the kids in the audience.

"They meet after school for an hour, Mondays and Wednesdays," Benny explained. "You can join two clubs, but you have to join at least one. So what are you interested in?"

"You don't have a skateboarding club, do you?" Zach asked, joking.

"Maybe *virtual* skateboarding," Benny said with a grin. "Nah, we've got chess and debating and forensics and chemistry — and of course computer club, which has about six branches. A lot of kids are into it. I could introduce you around."

"Cool!" Zach said. "I was going to say that computers are my second interest after boarding. I've been wanting to check out the school's equipment."

"Oh, man, it's awesome!" Benny enthused. "Wait till you see it!"

Zach was floored by what he saw in the school's huge computer room. All the latest equipment, with software to do anything you wanted. Full, fast Internet access and two faculty members who were experts on all of it!

The kids Benny introduced him to were all friendly. There was Bernard, of course, and Maurice, Enid, Tabitha, and Stuart. Nice kids, all of them — but if Brian Jeffers ever laid eyes on them, he'd fall over laughing. They looked as nerdy as could be.

"We thought you were a big snob when we saw you in the auditorium," Enid said. She had long, greasy hair and was about six feet tall, not counting her two-inch platform heels.

Her friend Tabitha, one of those kids who had been dressed by her parents, nodded in agreement. "You didn't talk to anybody this morning," she pointed out. "So everyone was saying you're stuck up. But you're not! That's so cool!"

"Yeah," Maurice said, a lock of his red hair falling over his eyes. "You're just the new kid on the block! Hahahaha!" Maurice had a weird laugh.

The newest nerd on the block, you mean, Zach said to himself. Great. Just great.

"So what's up with the hair and the pants?" Enid asked. "Are you trying to annoy your parents or something?"

Zach sighed. "You wouldn't understand," he said. He wasn't even sure *he* understood.

7

By the time he got home after Computer Club, it was four o'clock. Zoey was waiting for him on the front steps, with Lorena sitting next to her.

"Hi, Thack!" Lorena said with a big smile and a wave as he got off the late bus.

"Where have you been?" Zoey demanded. "I've been waiting and waiting for my lesson."

"Your lesson!" Zach said. "Sorry, I forgot."

"That's nice," Zoey said sarcastically. "I can still tell Mom and Dad about you and my piggy."

"No, Zoey, you don't need to do that."

"Fine. Let's start."

"Wait — wait now, I can't do it this minute."

"And why not?" she asked, her hands on her hips.

"I promised the guys I'd meet them at the park."

"So what? This is more important."

"To you, maybe."

Zoey narrowed her eyes. "I want my lesson — now — or I'm telling Mom and Dad everything."

Zach gritted his teeth and threw his backpack violently on the lawn. "Okay, okay!" he barked. "Let's get started. It's already late, and I don't have all afternoon. I'll give you half an hour."

"An hour."

"Okay, okay! Come on, let's go. Start putting on the pads."

"I still don't see why I have to wear all this stupid equipment," Zoey said as Zach tightened the helmet strap under her chin. "It doesn't even fit me."

"Neither does the board," Zach pointed out. "You ought to get yourself a smaller one."

"I don't have any money until you pay me back," she countered.

"Oh, yeah. Right." Not much he could say to that, Zach realized. He looked over at Lorena, who was still sitting on the steps at the side of the driveway. "Hey," he called to her. "Your parents need me to baby-sit anytime soon?"

"I dunno," Lorena said with a shrug. "Are you gonna give me a lethon, too?"

"You'll get a turn," he promised her.

"Thankth, Thack," she said, showing him her grin with the big dimples. "You're nithe."

Zach nodded and smiled, then picked up his board. "Now, this is the board," he began, showing it to them both.

"I know that already," Zoey said impatiently. "Lemme ride it!"

"Uh-uh-uh!" Zach cautioned, holding the board out of her reach. "First learn, then ride." He showed them both the different parts of the board — the deck, the trucks, the wheels, the skid plate, the kick tail, and the rail bar. "The rail bar is for doing grinds."

"What are grindth?" Lorena wanted to know.

"Sliding, kind of," Zach explained. "Like on a curb or a rail or the top of a ramp or half pipe."

"Oh."

"Here, I'll show you."

"No, *I* wanna do it!" Zoey said, holding firmly onto the board.

"You're not ready to do tricks yet. First, you —"

"First, I ride!" Zoey said.

"No — *first* you learn to *fall*," Zach said. "Then you ride."

"I know how to fall," Zoey insisted.

"Oh, yeah? How?" he asked.

"Like this!" Zoey flopped down on the pavement, and Lorena burst out laughing.

"Thoey, you are tho funny!" she sputtered hysterically. "Ithn't thee funny, Thack?"

"A riot," Zach said dryly. "Look, here's the two ways to fall. First, there's the forward roll." He demonstrated, tucking his head under as he fell forward, extending his arms out to guide his somersault.

"And here's the knee slide," he said. He took the knee pads from Zoey, snugged them into place, then ran three steps forward and slid onto his knees, gliding to a stop on his pads.

"Let me try, let me try!" Zoey begged.

"Okay, okay," he said, and put the pads on her knees. "There. Now you're all decked out. Helmet, elbow pads, wrist protectors, knee pads, sneakers. The works. Go!"

Zoey practiced falling, then let Lorena put on the equipment and have a turn.

"*Now* can I ride?" Zoey asked again.

"Next time," Zach put her off. "I've gotta go meet the guys at Moorehead Park."

"Oh, no you don't!" Zoey ordered. "Not till I've had my lesson!"

"You've had your lesson!"

"You call that a lesson? I haven't even ridden yet!"

"Me, neither!" Lorena echoed.

"Okay, okay," Zach grumbled, beaten. She had him over a barrel. He owed her, and she knew it.

So he stayed, even though he knew it was making him late. He stayed and taught them how to stand on the board, where to put their feet, and how to keep their weight low and forward. He taught them how to push off, how to maneuver their feet into riding position, and how to turn the board by leaning left and right. Finally, he showed them how to stop the board by dragging their back foot alongside it.

"Okay, that's all for today," he finally said. "Practice some more tomorrow and next time, I'll show you how to do wheelies and stuff."

"That was fun!" Zoey said happily. "I like falling the best."

"You sure did a lot of it," Zach quipped. "Hey, you'll like riding, too, once you get a little practice." He gave Zoey a smile. He'd actually enjoyed giving them a lesson. This wasn't going to be so bad after all.

"I like falling, too. Thankth, Thack!" Lorena said.

"Don't mention it," Zach said. "Okay, I'd better get going. It's already getting close to dinnertime."

Just then, he heard his mom ringing the dinner bell inside. "Already?" he cried. "What time is it?"

"Six-thirty," Zoey said, consulting her watch.

"That's impossible!" Zach cried. "Dang! I've already missed them!" Flinging down his helmet, he stormed into the house, on the verge of tears. That stupid Zoey! She'd made him miss seeing his friends!

"So where were you today, dude?"

"Huh? What? I can't hear you, Kareem. Hold on a second." Zach was on the telephone in the kitchen, taking a break from cleaning up after dinner. Behind him, his dad was loading the dishwasher, making a lot of noise. "Dad, could you cut it out a second? I'm on the phone."

"Oh. Sorry," his dad said with a sheepish smile, then mouthed the words *Who is it?*

Zach rolled his eyes and turned his back to his father. Like it was his parents' business whom he talked to! "There," he told Kareem. "Now what did you say?"

"I said, Where were you today after school?"

"Oh. I was . . ." Zach hesitated. He didn't want the guys to know he hadn't shown up because he was giving his little sister skateboarding lessons!

"I had to baby-sit," he fudged.

"Oh. Man, that bites. I hope you made good money."

"Yeah. I really needed to, after Saturday."

There was a pause on the other end of the line. "Saturday?"

"Yeah, you know, at the mall. I missed you guys there."

Another mysterious pause. "Uh, yeah. Well, anyway, are you coming to the park tomorrow?"

"Definitely. I've got to check out how you guys all look!"

"Uh, yeah. Well, see you then." Kareem hung up, and so did Zach, puzzled by the tone in his friend's voice. It was more than a little weird.

"I didn't know you were baby-sitting this afternoon," his dad said, surprised.

"That's because I wasn't," Zach said. "It's complicated."

"Oh. I see. Well, then," his dad said, rinsing another dish. "Come on, let's go back to work."

They finished rinsing the dishes and cleaning off the table and putting the leftovers in the fridge. "You haven't said much about your first day at school," his dad suddenly said.

"Oh. It was fine," Zach said, rinsing his hands in the sink.

"How were the facilities?"

"Great. Those were fantastic."

"Good!"

"Yeah, I guess." Zach heaved a sigh.

His dad regarded him for a long moment. "You don't seem very happy about it. Is there something I should know?"

"No, Dad," Zach said. He dried his hands on a dishtowel. "Like I said, it's complicated. You wouldn't understand."

He left the room, not wanting to see the hurt look in his father's eyes.

He endured the next day at Amherst, but it wasn't easy. Like the day before, most kids just stared at him, as if they couldn't get over how weird he looked. It was enough to drive Zach crazy. He was about ready to start staring back at them, with his mouth open like an idiot.

Luckily, lunchtime rolled around. He sat with the gang from Computer Club. But even among them, he was quiet and thoughtful. Something was bothering him . . . something about how Kareem had sounded on the phone the night before.

He couldn't wait to see the guys and get back among true friends. These nerdy kids were nice enough, but other than computers, what did he really have in common with them? He barely knew them.

He felt torn away from everything familiar, alone

in a strange new world. He paid no attention during his afternoon classes, and barely escaped ridicule when a teacher asked him a question he hadn't heard because he was daydreaming.

After school he went home and put on his gear. He checked himself out in the mirror. Somehow, he just couldn't get used to his new look. He didn't blame the kids at Amherst for giving him weird glances. He'd have done the same thing in their place.

Well, the hair was the hair. Nothing he could do about it. But the iron bar in his ear? It looked totally stupid.

The guy had said to wear it for forty-eight hours, to keep the hole open until it healed and stayed that way by itself. Well, it had to be forty-eight hours by now, Zach figured. Carefully, he twisted the bar open, and pulled it out of his ear.

There was no pain, to Zach's surprise. He could see the hole now, for the first time. It didn't look too bad. But without something in his ear, all there was to look at was his stupid hairstyle. The blond spikes would look okay on some of the other guys. But he didn't care what the hairstylist had said. They didn't look good on *him*.

He needed a really good earring for when the guys saw him. Brian already had that fake diamond stud. Zach wondered what the other guys would be wearing. Iron bars? He doubted it.

Now where could he get an earring in a hurry? Zach wondered. He perked up his ears and listened for the presence of someone in the house. Nothing. Mom and Dad were still at work, and Zoey was probably over at Lorena's.

Zach tiptoed into his parents' room and opened up his mom's vanity table. He examined the half dozen pairs of earrings lying in the top drawer, but none of them suited his purpose. They were all much too ladylike.

And then he remembered the small cubic zirconium studs he'd seen in Zoey's ears. They weren't for pierced ears, and they weren't really diamonds, though they did look like them. Zach decided one of the little clip-on studs would do nicely.

He'd have it back by dinnertime, and she'd never miss it. True, she'd discovered the missing money in a hurry, but that was different. Even if she missed the diamond, he could just give it to her and tell her he'd found it on the floor.

Confident that he was pulling off a harmless, easy little operation, he stole into Zoey's bedroom and quickly made off with one of her studs. He took a moment in front of the mirror to fasten it to his ear. Then he went outside, put on his gear, and pushed off for Moorehead Park.

He could see the guys at the far end of the playground as he skated toward the park entrance. They were in full gear, helmets glinting in the late-afternoon sun. They were practicing going down a flight of four steps one by one. It was a pretty hard trick to learn, and falls could be particularly painful if you happened to hit the sharp edge of a step with an unprotected part of your body.

As he passed through the park gate, Zach caught sight of a sign that read: MOOREHEAD PARK CLOSED FOR RENOVATIONS STARTING MONDAY, SEPTEMBER 12. WILL REOPEN NEXT SPRING. A PROJECT OF YOUR MUNICIPAL COUNCIL, JAMES T. TAYLOR, MAYOR.

"Next spring!" Zach gasped. "Why does it have to take so long to repave a stupid playground?"

He let out an exasperated groan. Where were they going to go now to practice? Today was

Wednesday. September 12 was next Monday. That left them only four more days after today!

He slalomed across the playground to join his friends. "Hey, you guys. Did you see the sign?" he called out to them.

"Yeah," Farrell said. "Can you believe it?"

"I'm gonna make my dad talk to the mayor," Sam said, his face hot with anger.

"What's your dad gonna do? Beat the mayor up?" Brian challenged him. All the kids laughed, except Sam and Zach. Zach knew he ought to laugh along, just to show he was one of the guys. But he couldn't manage it. He just didn't think making fun of poor little Sam was funny.

"Where are we gonna go?" Zach asked, looking at Brian, because he was always the one who decided things among them. "The sign said, 'closed till spring.'"

"We'll find someplace," Brian assured him.

"Okay, you guys," Zach said. "Let's see what everybody looks like." He removed his helmet, and let them see his new 'do.

Instead of the whoops and cheers and jokes he expected, he got stone-cold silence. "What?" he asked, his smile faltering as he saw his friends stealing guilty glances at one another. "What's going on?"

One by one, they removed their helmets. Sam, Kareem, Farrell, Jerry — not one of them had gone through with it!

"What the —! I can't believe you guys!" Zach felt the blood pounding in his ears again, and he knew his face had to be as red as a beet.

"We kind of chickened out at the last minute," Jerry admitted.

"We're gonna do it, though," Sam hurriedly assured him.

"Soon as we get the money together," Kareem put in. "See, our parents didn't want us to do it, so they wouldn't pay for it."

"Especially after what happened with the police," Farrell added. "Thank you, Brian."

"Shut up," Brian said. He skateboarded up to Zach and put a hand on his shoulder. "I'm proud of you, man. You're the first to do the dirty deed. Except for me, of course."

"Yeah," Zach said quietly, letting Brian give him their most elaborate, special handshake.

"It looks good on you, dude," Brian assured him.

"Yeah, thanks," Zach mumbled, unconvinced.

"Hey — I'm getting a tattoo next week," Brian told him. "You wanna come with me?"

"Um . . . maybe . . ."

"You're a true rebel, just like me," Brian told him with a slap on the back. "Not like the rest of these wusses."

"I'm getting a tattoo, too!" Sam insisted.

"Tattoo-tu-tu!" Brian mocked him, and everyone laughed — even Sam this time.

Zach didn't even crack a smile. He was furious with his friends for backing out and not telling him.

Everyone in his new school thought Zach was the biggest weirdo in the entire universe. On top of that, he now owed his little sister forty bucks, plus he had to give Zoey skateboarding lessons for two whole months! Sure, it had been fun the first time, but two months was going to be an eternity!

And for what! His so-called friends had hung him out to dry. They'd chickened out, and now he'd gone and made a total jerk out of himself!

And as if all that weren't bad enough, soon they weren't even going to be able to skateboard, because Moorehead Park was going to be closed till spring!

"So how's life at Geekhurst Academy?" Brian asked him.

"It's okay," Zach told him, staring at the broken pavement.

"Yeah, I'll bet you fit right in, too," Brian joked. Now the general laughter was being directed at Zach instead of at Sam.

"Like I said, it's pretty good. The computer stuff is awesome."

"Great. Yeah, well anyway . . ." Brian turned away, uninterested in hearing any more about Zach's school. He rode off, did an awesome grab over a fire hydrant, and made a soft, smooth landing.

"Hey, Zach, guess who Sam got for homeroom?" Farrell said.

"Who?"

"Sienkiewicz!"

"Get out of here! She's awesome."

"He is so lucky, isn't he? I swear, he's got every good teacher in sixth grade."

"Whose math class are you in, Simon?" Kareem asked Farrell.

"Sullivan's."

"Is he good?"

"He talks too fast . . . like this . . ." Farrell did an imitation of Mr. Sullivan, and Kareem laughed. Then Jerry joined in with a story about his chemistry teacher. Soon all the other boys were talking about life at Brighton Middle. "Ronnie Seifert likes Laura Osborne . . ." and "Richmond put a rotten egg in Freddie Barnes's locker. . . ."

Zach knew most of the kids they were talking about, but it all seemed far away somehow, as if he'd crossed a giant ocean to a distant shore.

"Did you see that incredible food fight in the cafeteria during lunch?" Jerry nudged Kareem, and both of them broke into hysterics.

"You had to be there," Jerry said to Zach apologetically. "It was a riot — literally!"

Zach tried to keep up, and even to throw in a comment once in a while. But he felt so sad, he almost wanted to cry. It was his old life they were talking about — a life he'd never get back again.

Finally, he couldn't take any more. He pushed off on his board and started practicing some of his freestyle tricks. He tick-tacked across the pavement, did a few wheelies and one or two pretty good ollies.

When it was time to leave, Zach boarded home alone, full of bitterness and regret.

Why had his parents transferred him away from his friends? Why had he gone and bleached his hair without making sure his friends had done it, too? And how was he going to fit in at his new school?

He stopped inside the front door of his house to check himself out one last time in the hall mirror, and gasped in horror. His earring — Zoey's "diamond" stud — was *gone!*

"Oh, great. This is just great!" Zach said, smacking his forehead with the palm of his hand. "*Now* what am I gonna do?"

He would have retraced his steps back to Moorehead Park, but it was already too dark outside. And tomorrow morning, while he was at school, some preschooler running around Moorehead Park would probably pick up the earring and swallow it.

Man, Zoey was going to kill him when she found out. He was cooked. Toast.

History.

"Wait a minute," he suddenly thought aloud. "She'll never know I stole it. It could have fallen on the floor and gotten vacuumed up or something. It could have fallen out of Zoey's ear!"

He was safe, Zach reassured himself. No way could this ever come back to haunt him.

"It's her fault anyway," he told himself. "If she'd had the guts to get her ears pierced, that earring wouldn't have been the clip-on kind. They fall out much easier."

Of course, he'd have to go buy Zoey a new pair as soon as he got enough money, and give them to her as a present. That way, he wouldn't feel so guilty about "borrowing" the earring and losing it.

Meanwhile, though, he had to have an earring. He needed one for school tomorrow. Without it, his hair looked totally wack. "Oh, well," he mused as he snuck into his sister's room. "One earring's no good to Zoey anyway. And two could have gotten lost just as easily as one."

I've been meaning to ask you," Benny Santangelo said as they sat together over lunch. "Is that your real hair?"

Zach laughed so hard that the milk he was drinking squirted out of his nose. "Quit it! You're gonna make me ruin my clothes!" he told Benny, wiping himself off with a paper napkin as he tried to stop laughing.

"Seriously, is it?"

"Stop!"

"Okay, okay. But . . . well, what were you thinking when you decided to get that done to yourself?"

"I don't know what I was thinking," Zach confided, sighing miserably. "To tell you the truth, I'm about ready to shave it off and start from scratch again."

Benny nodded, then said in a deadpan voice, "I'd suggest using one of those hair-removal products. It'll hurt less than a razor, and it'll grow back slower."

Zach blinked. It took him a second to realize Benny was joking around with him. Then he cracked up again. "You're a sick man, dude," he said, giving Benny a high five and a smile. "Seriously, though, I'm not gonna shave my head, one way or the other."

"No, that wouldn't be good," Benny agreed. "You'd look just as weird."

"Weirder."

"And all that trouble for nothing." Benny thought for a minute. "I guess you're stuck with it until it grows out a little. Then you can get a buzz cut and start fresh. . . . Or . . ."

"Or what?"

"Or you could go to the store, buy a rinse, and color your hair so it looks like normal."

Zach considered this for a moment. "What about the spikes?" he asked.

"You'd want to try cutting them off, I guess," Benny said with a shrug.

"I don't know how good a job I could do of it,"

Zach said. "I might make a real mess of my hair, and then I'd *have* to shave my head."

"If you ask me," Benny said, "it's worth the risk. Look, you said none of your friends had the guts to bleach their hair. So you're the only one who wound up looking like a space alien."

"There's one kid, Brian, he was the first to do it. But I don't know . . . it looks good on him, somehow. It fits him."

"He's a space alien?"

Zach laughed. "Kind of. Anyway, you're right. If they didn't have the guts to do it, why should I keep my hair like this? I guess I'll try the rinse-and-hack method."

"Sounds like a plan," Benny said. "Er, what about the earring?"

"What about it?" Zach asked. "I like the earring."

"Oh. Okay," Benny backed off. "That's cool, I guess. It would be better if it wasn't a clip-on."

"Dang! Is it that obvious?" Zach moaned.

"Only close up," Benny replied from across the table. "From a distance, it's very convincing. And I'm sure it's less obvious under a skateboarding helmet."

"It is," Zach assured him. "Definitely."

"Now . . . ahem," Benny said, clearing his throat. "The, er, pants . . . ?" He pointed discreetly at Zach's wide-leg jeans and shook his head disapprovingly. "Lose 'em."

"Yeah, right," Zach said with a grin. "I should walk around here in my underwear."

"You know what I mean," Benny insisted. "Don't you have any normal pants? Those would fit me, but on you, they're ridiculous."

"It's the kind skateboarders wear," Zach explained.

"So wear them skateboarding," Benny suggested. "All the kids are getting a good laugh out of them. If you want to be the subject of everybody's jokes . . ."

"So what am I supposed to do about it?" Zach demanded. "All my jeans are like this!"

"You know," Benny said, eyeing the jeans, "those things shrink if you wash and dry them on high heat. You might want to try *altering* a few pairs — as an experiment."

"I can't believe I'm getting fashion advice from you, of all people," Zach shook his head in dismay.

But the more he thought about "altering" his jeans, the more he liked the idea.

He started pacing back and forth across his room — which was not easy to do. He had to kick aside all the clothes he'd tossed on the floor during the previous week and never picked up.

There were his three new pairs of skateboarding jeans — the kind with the wide legs all the way down. He'd had to really battle with his parents to get them to buy him those jeans. And now that he was going to Amherst, he looked like a total geek wearing them to school. Benny was right — those three pairs of jeans were ripe for "alteration." And he'd still have the pair he was wearing for skateboarding.

He knew his parents would never agree to buying him new, tighter-fitting jeans for Amherst. He could just hear them now. "We're not made out of money," his dad would say.

And his mom: "Those jeans we bought you in July are still practically new. Don't be such a slave to fads and fashions!"

Zach grabbed the three pairs of jeans and went downstairs. In the laundry room he put them into the washing machine, set the water temperature for extra hot, and started the washer.

There. That and about two hours in the dryer on high heat should just about do it, he figured. He'd have three brand new pairs of narrow-leg jeans, just right for Amherst Academy.

"Zachary! What in the world did you do to your new jeans?!" His mom looked horrified as she held up pair after pair, now shrunken pitifully, way beyond even tight-leg size.

"I . . . I guess I messed up doing the laundry," Zach said. "I thought they were pre-shrunken, so I put them in on high heat."

"Oh, my goodness . . ." His mom shook her head in dismay. "I don't know what is the matter with you, Zachary Halper. But your father is going to go ballistic when I tell him you need new jeans again. We just bought these for you."

"But I *need* new ones, Mom!" Zach begged, feeling guilty now. "Even you can see that!"

"I don't see why I shouldn't just make you wear

these," his mother said, frowning. "You could probably still wear them, if you fastened them with a big safety pin."

"Mom!" Zach shouted, his voice cracking pathetically. "Give those to Zoey! You have to buy me new clothes!"

"I don't have to do anything, young man, and neither does your father. I'll speak with him, and we'll see what he says. Meanwhile, you just wait in your room."

Zach stormed upstairs, furious at his parents and at himself. If they didn't cave in, he was going to be down to a single pair of skateboarding jeans: the pair he had on right now — in fact, the ones he'd worn yesterday, too. How many days in a row could he wear one pair of jeans? Good grief!

His mom knocked on the door of his room, then came in without his permission.

"Your father says you can have one new pair of pants and that's it," she told him. "Considering the way you've been behaving, I think that's more than fair."

"Thanks, Mom," Zach murmured, barely audible. "Sorry I ruined my jeans."

And he was, too. He was sorry about everything: sorry he'd bleached and spiked his hair, sorry he'd taken his sister's money, sorry he'd lost her earring, sorry he'd stolen the other one, sorry he'd ruined his jeans, sorry he'd gone to Amherst — sorry he'd ever been born!

In the end, he went for a pair of khakis. It was what the kids at Amherst mostly wore anyway. Besides, they were on sale, leaving him enough money for a bottle of hair-coloring rinse.

He still had his one pair of wide-leg jeans to go skateboarding with. Plus all his sweatpants. It would have to last him until Christmas. But at least he could get his hair back to normal.

When he got home, he went straight into the bathroom and locked the door. He followed the instructions on the bottle, and fifteen minutes later his hair was something like its usual brown color. Zach then took a big scissors, and cut the spikes out of his hair as best he could.

In the end, it didn't look too bad. Kind of uneven on top where the spikes had been, but all things considered, it could have been much worse. Zach got dressed in his wide-legs and T-shirt. It was time to give Zoey her second skateboarding lesson.

But first, he returned the second earring to the nightstand where it had been before he "borrowed" it. Even though he liked the way it looked on him, he didn't need it for school anymore. Besides, the last thing he needed was for Zoey to see it in his ear, notice the resemblance to her own earrings, and then go looking for them.

"There," he said, putting the earring back just the way he'd found it. "That's one thing I won't have to worry about anymore."

"Okay, kick — turn!" Zach instructed. "Good!"

Zoey beamed a brilliant smile back at him. For the last hour, he'd been teaching her and Lorena how to do different kinds of turns. He'd set up a series of obstacles for them to zigzag around. When he'd paid Zoey back for everything, he'd go out and buy some real cones, he told himself. It would be worth it to make a real skateboarding course right here in the driveway. Maybe he could even scare up some plywood for a ramp!

"My turn, Thack!" Lorena called out.

"Okay, Lorena. Zoey, take off the pads and stuff."

"I'm not done practicing yet!" Zoey protested.

"Come on, Zoey, give her a turn. She's your friend."

"Oh, okay." Zoey turned over the gear to Lorena and sat next to Zach on the steps.

"You look much better this way," she offered.

"Yeah, right," Zach said, scowling.

"You do. I don't care what you think," she said. "And you know what else? You're a good teacher."

He looked up at her, just to make sure she was serious. "Thanks," he said, smiling.

"By the time two months is over, I'm going to be a better skateboarder than you and your friends," Zoey bragged.

"We'll see about that," Zach said with a laugh. "Whoa, Lorena! Remember to tuck your head under when you fall!"

"I'm okay," Lorena said, picking herself up off the pavement. "How do you do that kick turn again?

Just then, Zach saw a sight that chilled his blood. His friends were skateboarding around the corner, calling his name and whooping loudly. If they caught him giving his little sister skateboarding lessons, they'd never let him hear the end of it.

"Quick, Lorena — give me all the gear!"

"Why, Thack?"

"Never mind why, just give it to me!"

"Halper!"

"Hey, guys!" Zach turned and waved to his friends as they approached. At the same time, he grabbed the board, and turned his back on Zoey and Lorena, hoping they'd have the good sense to get lost in a hurry.

The smile vanished from Zach's face as he got a good look at his buddies. They had all bleached and spiked their hair!

"Oh, no!" he groaned.

"We did it!" Sam crowed. "I told you we'd do it! Hey, how come you got rid of it, Zach?"

"I got tired of it," Zach muttered weakly. "I figured you guys chickened out, so . . ."

"Yeah, well now you're gonna have to go get it done again," Kareem said. "Gotta look like a crew."

"I'm not getting it done again," Zach said. "Sorry. You all should have done it when you said you would. So too bad."

"You all look stupid," Zoey piped up, stepping forward. "Why do you all want to look so freaky?"

"This your sister?" Brian Jeffers asked.

"Uh, yeah," Zach said, wishing he could make Zoey disappear — and Lorena along with her. "Yeah, this is Zoey. She's nine. And that's her friend Lorena. I'm . . . I'm baby-sitting them," he fibbed.

"Oh. Gotta make some ducats, huh?" Brian said with a wink and a nod.

"He's not baby-sitting us!" Zoey contradicted. "We're not babies!"

"Quiet, Zoey!" Zach said through gritted teeth. But it was too late. All the guys cracked up.

"Yeah, we're big girlth," Lorena added. "Thack's giving uth thkateboarding lethonth."

Oh brother, Zach thought. *That's all I need. Now they're gonna be imitating poor Lorena's lisp all afternoon.*

"Oh, that'th tho thweet!" Brian mimicked, drawing a huge roar from the other boys.

"Shut up, Brian," Zach scolded him, putting his arm around Lorena's shoulder to comfort her. He could see the tears already forming in her eyes.

"Thack'th nithe," she told Brian. "Not like you. You're not nithe at all!"

"Tho thorry," Brian joked, starting another round of laughter.

Lorena, bawling, broke free of Zach and ran into the house.

"There. Are you happy now?" Zach said to Brian. "You made her cry. Nice going."

"Oh, Thack!" Brian said, still not done. "You're tho thenthitive!"

Zach gave him a little shove. "Cut it out," he warned.

Brian smirked. "It must be the Amherst Academy effect," he said. "Makes you all soft and gooey and nerdy inside, so you want to spend all your time with little girls."

"Shut up, I said," Zach muttered threateningly. "I had to give them lessons, okay? I had no choice."

"Oh? And why not?" Brian wondered.

"I . . . borrowed some money from Zoey," Zach said, motioning with his eyes toward Zoey, who was still there in the driveway watching the confrontation. "For the haircut and the ear piercing."

"Yeah, right," Brian said. "Don't give me that baloney. You didn't even get your ear pierced."

Zach drew back, surprised. "I did too," he said. "Here — see?"

Brian examined the hole in Zach's ear. "Oh," he said. "So you did. My mistake."

"That's right," Zach said, nodding to show he was righteously offended.

"See, I just figured since you were using a clip-on earring, you hadn't done the dirty deed."

"A-a clip-on earring?" Zach stammered.

"Yeah. You dropped it at Moorehead Park. Here. I kept it for you." He handed Zach the diamond stud.

Zoey's eyes went wide, and she came closer to get a better look. "Hey!" she cried. "That's *my* earring! Zach, you thief! You stole my earring, too!"

"Whoa, dude!" Brian said laughing so hard, he could barely stand. "You're wearing your little sister's jewelry now?" He backed up, exchanging humorous glances with the other guys. "Okay, I'm outie. Come on guys. See you sometime, Zach, huh?" They all skateboarded off, leaving Zach there in a state of total humiliation.

But the worst was yet to come.

"I'm telling!" Zoey shrieked, running inside before Zach could stop her. "Mommy! Daddy! Zach stole my money and my earring! He let the other boys make fun of me! Mommy! Daddy!"

Zach sank to the pavement and sat there, his head in his hands. "This is it," he said to himself. "This is what they mean when they say, 'You've hit rock bottom.'"

It was the beginning of a long, painful month for Zach. His parents grounded him until he repaid Zoey all the money he'd taken from her piggy bank. They forbade him to go skateboarding without Zoey, which pretty much meant he was confined to the driveway and the sidewalk of their block.

Kareem called once, to say the boys were hanging out in back of the A&P, whose parking lot was so big that part of it was always empty. It wasn't as good a layout as Moorehead Park; aside from some curbs and a couple of speed bumps, there wasn't much in the way of obstacles. But at least the pavement was better, and until they fixed Moorehead Park, it was the only game in town.

Zach explained why he couldn't go. Kareem sympathized, but after that, there wasn't much to talk about, so they hung up quickly. And that was the last he'd heard from any of them — three weeks ago.

He'd done a lot of baby sitting in that time. Lorena's parents had given his name to some friends of theirs who needed help Friday and Saturday nights. He'd spent the afternoons giving the girls lessons. They could now actually ride their boards.

Zoey had already extracted a skateboard from their parents as an early birthday present. Lorena was working on her parents to do the same for her, and it seemed that she wouldn't have too hard a time getting one, even though her birthday wasn't till just before Thanksgiving.

Zach had splurged on some cones for them to work with. It had set him back a day of baby-sitting wages, but he didn't care anymore. It gave him a chance to set up different slalom courses in the driveway.

His skills were actually getting better with all this practice. Even though most of the tricks he tried were really easy, he was getting so good at them that he could put together a few at a time, which enabled him to create routines on the board.

One day he brought his boom box outside and

gave his routine some background music. Zoey and Lorena really enjoyed the addition of a sound track to their boarding activities. They were each improving steadily and were certainly no longer embarrassing.

Outside of giving the girls lessons, the only good things in Zach's life were his technology classes and Computer Club at Amherst. They were really interesting, and he'd learned a lot. And with his hair and clothing close to what Amherst kids considered normal, he was slowly making friends, although none as close as Benny Santangelo.

One day Benny and he were sitting next to each other in computer engineering class, when the teacher handed out a series of sheets detailing their big end-of-semester assignment.

"You'll be working in teams," Mr. Schmidt said. "You'll have to come up with a detailed computer design of a structure with moving parts."

"What kind of structure?" one of the kids asked.

"That's entirely up to you," the teacher said. "It could be a drawbridge or an elevator for a building. Try to be creative. But I'll expect a two-page written report explaining how you came up with it and how it works."

"Cool!" Benny said, turning to powwow with Zach. "Got any good ideas?"

Zach shrugged. "You're the idea man," he said. "Just one request."

"What?"

"We work at your house. I need to get away," Zach said, rolling his eyes. "I'm in prison at my house."

"No problem," Benny assured him. "I'll have my mom call your mom and set it up." He winked at Zach, and they shook on it.

That evening Zach's mom was about to drive him to Benny's for a brainstorming session on their big project when the phone rang. His mom went into the kitchen to answer it.

"Skeeter, hi!" Zach heard her say, greeting his uncle. "How are you? How's the weather out in sunny California?" She listened, and then said, "Well, I'm just driving Zach over to a friend's house."

There was a pause. Zach tapped on the back of the sofa impatiently.

Then he heard his mom say, "Oh, we're surviving, I guess. Things have been tense with us. . . ."

Zach knew she was talking about him. He could

tell by the hush that came into her voice. He edged over to the open kitchen door, to hear better.

"He just doesn't seem to want to play by the rules," his mom was complaining. "We can't do anything with him. Do you know the police brought him home one night? And Zoey caught him stealing from her piggy bank, can you believe it? Oh, Skeeter, you have such a way with kids. Maybe if you had a little talk with him? Everything we say just goes in one ear and out the other."

Zach, hiding on the other side of the kitchen door, felt a sudden urge to sneeze come over him. He tried to stifle it, but it was too late. "Aaah-choo!!!"

His mom, hearing him, broke off the conversation. "I'll call you back later," she told Skeeter, and hung up. "Were you listening in, Mr. Sneak?" she asked Zach as she came out into the living room.

"Listening to what?" Zach asked innocently.

His mom frowned, but didn't say anything else until they were in the car driving to Benny's. Then she said, "That was your uncle Skeeter on the phone."

"Oh, yeah?" Zach said flatly. He loved his uncle Skeeter, who was one of the most fun adults he'd ever met. But right now he couldn't muster much excitement for anything.

"He sends his regards."

"That's nice."

His mom sighed, and shook her head. "What time shall I pick you up?" she asked.

"I'll call you." Zach got out and went up the steps to ring Benny's doorbell. He didn't look back as the car drove away.

"Well?" Benny asked him as he let Zach in.

"Well, what?" Zach asked.

"Any ideas for our project?"

"Nope. You?"

"Not a one," Benny pushed his broken, taped-up glasses onto the bridge of his nose. "But I did come up with a cool program for simulating whatever we wind up making. Wanna see?"

"Cool!" Zach smiled and followed Benny down into the basement, where the Santangelo family had their computer desk set up. Benny called up the program he'd written.

"Say you wanted to do a bridge," he began, and showed Zach how, by entering just a few commands, he could create the bridge, see it from any angle, and even make it sway in an imaginary wind.

"That's incredible!" Zach said. "You did that yourself?"

Benny shrugged. "It was easy," he said.

"Yeah, right. Man, we are gonna get an A-plus!" He high-fived Benny, but then their smiles began to fade. "We still need an idea," Zach said. "We could do a bridge, I guess."

"Uh-uh," Benny said, shaking his head. "Bernard and Enid are doing a bridge together. They'd clean our clocks. Bernard is a genius, and Enid's smarter than he is."

"What about an elevator or something?"

"Nah. Everyone in class will be doing that," Benny told him. "But my program isn't limited to buildings, see. We can do anything — a spaceship, maybe?"

"That's not a bad idea," Zach said. "Kind of corny, though . . ."

"Yeah, I guess you're right," Benny agreed reluctantly. "So what do we do now?"

"I guess we sit around until we get the idea we want to do, and then you program it in for us."

Benny made a face. "I think you should come up with the idea then, Zach. It's only fair."

"But I can't think of anything!" Zach complained. "My brain needs a break. What else do you have to do around here?" Zach looked around the basement, examining Mr. Santangelo's weights and Mrs. Santangelo's treadmill.

Then he opened a little wooden door, and gasped. "Wow! What a cool workshop!"

Zach had always liked shop class at school. He was good at making things, and the projects he did invariably got A's. But his parents weren't handy at all, and the tools they kept around the house were totally lame. So Zach never really got much of a chance to exercise his talents in woodworking.

The Santangelos, on the other hand, had an incredible workshop set up in their basement. There was a huge worktable, with saws, a lathe, and other power tools. On a pegboard along one wall were all kinds of hand tools. Sheets of plywood were stacked against the far wall, and more lumber was piled in bins in one corner.

"My dad likes to do wood projects," Benny

explained. "He built our deck last year, and now he's working on an addition to the family room. Mom always complains about all that scrap lumber, but she sure loves the finished project when it's done!"

"Scrap lumber?" An idea suddenly came to him. "Hey, Benny, do you think I could use some of this plywood and those tools to make a skateboarding ramp for my driveway?"

"Well, this stuff isn't mine," Benny pointed out. "It's my dad's. And my dad doesn't let anybody work without supervision."

"Oh," Zach said, disappointed.

"Of course, if I asked him nicely, he'd probably come down and help us."

"Really?" Zach asked, his jaw dropping.

"Nope," Benny said with a smile. "He just loves to work with wood. It's what he does for a hobby, and he loves it when I do it with him. Kind of like a father-and-son thing."

"That's phat. Oh, man, I hope he says yes. A ramp in the driveway would be so cool!" Zach mused. He told Benny about the cones he'd put out. "It would make my skateboarding course complete."

Benny turned to the computer and logged on to

the Internet. "Let's just see if we can download some building plans for a ramp and go find Dad!"

Three hours later, when his mom came to pick him up, Zach was standing in Benny's driveway. Next to him was a curved wooden ramp made out of plywood. "Hi, Mom!" He waved to her.

"What's this, Zachary?" she asked him, getting out of the car.

"Benny's dad's giving me this ramp," he told her. "It's for skateboarding tricks in the driveway."

"Well, isn't that nice of him!" his mom said with a smile. "I'm so glad you're making such nice new friends at Amherst." Then she cleared her throat. "Of course, Zoey is not to go anywhere near that thing, do you understand?"

"Of course not, Mom!" Zach said, rolling his eyes. "Do I look that stupid?"

"All right, all right," she said. "Come on, let's get this thing in the back."

They managed to lift the ramp between them. It just fit in the back of the station wagon. As they drove off toward home, his mom asked, "So what did you two boys come up with?"

"Uh, nothing," Zach said lamely.

His mother's mouth grew tight. "What do you mean, nothing? I drove you over here so you could work on your project. Did you do any work at all?"

"We tried, Mom," Zach explained defensively. "But neither of us could think of anything good."

"I'm sure," his mother said, making a face. "You probably just played video games or watched TV."

"Whatever you say, Mom." Zach stared out the window. He sure wasn't going to volunteer the information that they'd spent their homework time building a skateboarding ramp.

"Look, young man," she said, pulling into their driveway and stopping the car, "you are still officially grounded until you work off your debt to your sister. Since you're obviously taking advantage of our good nature, next time you and your partner can work on your project here at our house."

Zach clucked his tongue and got out of the car without answering her. What was the use, anyway?

As he came into the house, the phone rang. Zach picked up the extension. "Hello?" he said.

"Zach? It's your uncle Skeeter, dude!"

"Oh, hey, Skeeter," Zach said grudgingly. "You want to talk to Mom again?"

"Actually, I called to talk to you, partner," Skeeter said, in that hippie twang of his. Skeeter had once been an actual hippie — living on a commune in northern California for two years after dropping out of college. Later he'd gotten work harvesting giant sequoia and redwood pinecones by climbing hundreds of feet up into the great old trees. On one of those climbs, he'd taken a fall of over a hundred feet and broken nearly every bone in his body.

Skeeter had recovered much better than anyone could have hoped, but he never got back to having what Zach's parents would have called a "normal life." He now lived in Venice, California, in a little house just off the beach and the boardwalk. Zach had no idea how his uncle got by, since according to Zach's mom, he never had a job.

Still, Zach really liked Skeeter. Normally he would have been happy to talk to him. But right now Zach was in a pretty foul mood. He knew the reason Skeeter wanted to talk with him was that Zach's mom had asked him to.

"I gotta go do something right now," Zach said.

"Okay, this'll only take a minute, dude," Skeeter said quickly, not letting Zach off the hook. "Look,

I've got lots of space out here, and not a lot of company, so I was wondering if you'd maybe want to come out and visit me over Columbus Day weekend. We could spend some time hanging out, and I could show you the scene out here. It's pretty incredible."

"Sounds okay," Zach said. "But I don't know if I —"

"There's a big skateboarding exhibition gonna happen on the boardwalk," Skeeter said, tempting him. "Professionals from all over the country."

"For real?" Zach gasped, forgetting his reluctance.

"I know some of these dudes from the old days," Skeeter said. "I could introduce you. You might even pick up a pointer or two, assuming you're not already a super hotshot yourself."

Zach laughed. "Okay. I guess I could make it."

"Excellent!" Skeeter said, in his Valley-guy surfer-dude voice. "And bring your board, dude. It's gonna be a party on wheels!"

11

On the Thursday before Columbus Day weekend, Zach finally paid Zoey back the last of the money he owed her. He even had a few dollars left over.

Feeling confident that his parents would give him some money to spend in California, he decided to celebrate by spending his few extra dollars on a sundae at the Ice Cream Parlor, down by Foley Square.

He rode his skateboard over there, sat down on one of the old-fashioned swivel stools by the bar, and ordered the house special sundae — chocolate ice cream with fudge and strawberry sauce, topped with whipped cream and sprinkles.

He was just digging into it when who should come into the place but Brian Jeffers. "Hey, Halper! Long time, no see!" He came over to Zach and put a hand on his shoulder. "Que pasa, man? What you been up to? Still playing with your little sister?"

"I've been grounded, okay?" Zach shot back. "I had to give Zoey lessons till I paid back the money I took from her."

"Oh, yeah? I notice you're out and about."

"I paid it off today."

"Cool! So now you're free to come boarding again?"

"That's right."

"Too bad Moorehead Park's all torn up. There's no place else in this stupid town to board. The A&P lot really stinks."

"Actually, you should check out my driveway. I've got it all set up," Zach told him.

"Yeah, right. Your driveway."

"No, listen, it's really working. It's long and pretty wide, and I put out cones and a ramp, too."

"A ramp? Where'd you buy a ramp?"

"I didn't buy one. I made it."

"Yeah, right, you made a ramp."

"I did, with my friend Benny and his dad."

"Benny? You've got a friend named Benny?"

"Yeah. Benny Santangelo. What's wrong with that?"

"Benny Santangelo. Sounds like a gangster."

Zach laughed in spite of himself. "He's pretty cool."

"Pretty cool for a nerd, you mean."

"I'd like to see you make a ramp as good as the one he made," Zach challenged.

"It's pretty good, huh?"

"I'm telling you, you've gotta try it. The cones are phat, too."

"Okay, we'll come down," Brian said. He ordered two scoops to go, then said, "Guess what?"

"What?"

"I'm getting my tattoo tomorrow." Brian flashed him a conspiratorial grin. "Right here." He pointed to his left bicep. "It's gonna be a skateboard, flying through the air, with the word *ragin'* written on it."

"Ragin', huh? Cool," Zach said, staring at his sundae to avoid Brian's gaze.

"You gonna get one, too?" he asked Zach. "All the other guys are doing it."

"They're all getting the same one?"

"Uh-huh." Brian shrugged. "Unless you've got a better idea."

"No, that one sounds good," Zach said, nodding.

Inside, he could feel his heart hammering in his chest. Tattoos hurt a lot, he knew. All those needles puncturing you. And they sometimes got infected. . . . And they were part of you *forever.*

Zach had already been burned once, bleaching his hair. This time, he decided, he would wait to see if the others went ahead with getting tattoos. After all, this was the first time one of his old friends had spoken to him for a long time. How was he to know for sure if they were really going to go through with it? He still wanted to be a part of their crew — after all, they were the skateboard renegades of Moorehead City — but it wouldn't hurt to be the last one to get tattooed.

"Wanna come with us and get it done, all of us together?" Brian asked.

Then Zach remembered, with a huge rush of relief, that he had a perfect excuse. "I can't," he said. "I'm going out to California for the holiday, to visit my uncle."

"My condolences," Brian told him, assuming Zach didn't want to be going. "Well, we'll all meet you Tuesday after school, then. Four o'clock — your driveway?"

"I'll be there," Zach told him.

"Great," Brian said, paying for his ice cream and heading for the door. "We'll check out your skateboard course, and then we can all board down here to Foley Square, and get you tattooed like the rest of us!"

Zach thought about that tattoo all the way to Los Angeles International Airport. Only the sight of his uncle Skeeter in the terminal took his mind off the prospect of getting hundreds of needle pricks in his arm.

Skeeter had straight blond hair, done in braids that reached all the way down his back. His dancing eyes were light green — so light that they looked almost yellow, like a cat's eyes. He wore a floppy black hat with a rainbow-colored feather in it, a woven Mexican vest with fringes, and big shorts that went way down below his knees. Old, torn sneakers topped off the look.

Skeeter looked like a bum — or an old hippie or a retro fashion statement — depending on how you looked at it. Zach glanced around the airport, a little embarrassed when Skeeter gave him a big hug in greeting.

"How're you doin', big guy! Whoa, look at you, dude. You are seriously big."

Zach smiled shyly. "I grew four inches this year already," he told his uncle.

"Is that all the stuff you brought?" Skeeter asked, pointing at Zach's duffel.

"Uh-huh."

"Where's the board?"

"In the bag."

Skeeter nodded, grinning. "Cool. Let's be off then, amigo." He led Zach outside to a bus stop.

"We're taking the bus?" Zach asked in amazement.

"I don't drive," Skeeter said.

"Why not?" Zach asked. "Was it the accident?"

"Well, obviously I stopped after that, yeah," Skeeter replied. "But that isn't mainly why. I just got tired of contributing to air pollution and the destruction of the rain forests."

"Yeah, but one more car isn't going to mean that much," Zach pointed out, unhappy at having to take public transportation in a city where having a cool car is as much a part of the scene as breathing.

"Ah, that's not the point, though," Skeeter said as

the bus arrived and they got on. "Either I'm a part of the solution or a part of the problem. I figure if I want to feel at home in my own skin, I've got to be part of the solution as much as I can. Over the year in the hospital and rehab, while all my bones were mending, I found out I could live without the four-wheeled vehicles. I skateboard all around Venice. It's cool. Everybody skates there or runs or bikes. You don't need a car — trust me."

They had to transfer buses to get to Venice Beach, north of the airport, where Skeeter had his bungalow.

"These were beach bungalows for the movie people back in the day," Skeeter told Zach as they walked down the pedestrian lanes of Venice.

Zach could hear the distant sound of the surf hitting the beach. "This is such a cool place!" he enthused.

"You ain't seen nothin' yet, dude," Skeeter promised as he opened the unlocked door of his bungalow.

Inside, the place was small, dark, and cool in the midday heat. There wasn't much furniture, Zach noticed, but there sure was a lot of other unusual stuff. Native American artifacts were scattered here and there. Several clay flutes were laid out on a worktable, some of them still unpainted. Sculptures of animals made from folded dollar bills decorated the mantelpiece. And there was a whole room full of skateboards!

"What in the world are you doing with all these?" Zach gasped. Some of the boards were decorated in fantastic, futuristic colors. There were old-fashioned ones as well as new models Zach had never seen.

"I fix people's boards," Skeeter explained. "Repair them, decorate them. It's a living — if you live like I do, that is. Meaning it's not much of one."

"That's your job?" Zach asked, awestruck.

"One of my jobs," Skeeter said. "I've got a few. But they're all pretty cool. You'll see."

"But . . . why'd you ask me to bring my board with me?" Zach wondered.

"Because, dude, I want to see what you ride on. How else are we gonna jazz up your act?"

Zach was totally blown away. He had thought he was coming out here to get a lecture, by way of his parents, delivered by good old uncle Skeeter. He hadn't believed his mom's cover story — that he was going to be having the time of his life skateboarding — until now.

"Can we go out boarding right away?" Zach asked.

"After lunch," Skeeter said. "Gotta charge the old batteries. You like sprouts?"

Zach swallowed hard. "Sprouts?"

"Alfalfa or bean. They're excellent, dude. You're gonna love 'em. And they love you, too."

When Zach first saw the Venice boardwalk, he thought he'd died and gone to heaven. It was made of pavement and was more of a promenade than a boardwalk. But it was more than either of those. It was a *show*.

Street performers were out in force on this Saturday of a three-day weekend. There were mimes, jugglers, magicians, a fire-eater, and lots of guys with guitars playing music.

Crowds of people passed by the performers, stopping to watch and listen, or hurrying on, walking, jogging, skating, boarding, biking, running, dancing, unicycling. The mood was good, with everybody seeming happy on this golden, sunny day.

"Tune into the *chi*, dude!" Skeeter said, as he boarded down the promenade right behind Zach. "Go with the flow!"

He caught up to Zach, and Zach got a look at the way Skeeter danced on his board, his whole body bouncing to the music of the street performers. Skeeter skidded into a wheelie, then ran off seven or eight 360 turns in a row, spinning like a champion ice skater. Everyone applauded, and Skeeter tipped his black feathered hat.

Zach smiled and shook his head. He wondered how his mom and Skeeter had gotten along growing up together. They sure were different!

"Hey, Skeeter!" some of the street performers waved as the two of them skateboarded by. "How's it goin'?"

"Excellent!" Skeeter called back. "Rock on!"

He turned to Zach. "What do you think, dude?"

"It's awesome!" Zach acknowledged.

"When your mom told me you were boarding, I knew you had to come out here and see this place. Wait till you see the boarding park, where they're doing the exhibition. Ramps? Half pipes? Dude, they have it all."

"Did you get us tickets?" Zach asked.

"Tickets? Amigo, we don't need tickets. I'm in the competition."

"What?"

"Your uncle's got game, kid," Skeeter said with a wink, and hopped into a handstand on his board!

"Wow!" Zach gasped.

Skeeter spun it around for a few 360s before coming down to earth again.

"That is so awesome!" Zach said giddily. "Man, I am soooo glad I came here."

"Dude," Skeeter said, putting an arm across Zach's shoulders, "so am I."

That night they sat on the low concrete wall that faced the beach and the ocean, and watched the sun go down and the stars come up.

"Mom and Dad think I'm the worst kid in the world," Zach was saying, staring out at the ocean as he talked. Skeeter sat next to him, with his arms around his knees, his eyes fixed on the fading light to the west. "They think my friends are future criminals or something."

"And they're not," Skeeter said softly.

115

"No, they're not!" Zach retorted. "They're just kids. They're supposed to be immature sometimes, right? They're not perfect, and neither am I. But that doesn't make me a criminal."

"No," Skeeter agreed. "That doesn't make you a criminal. Stealing, that's a crime."

Zach sneaked a glance at him. Was Skeeter talking about how he'd stolen from Zoey's piggy bank or taken her earrings? Or did he just mean stealing in general? From Skeeter's tone of voice, it was hard to tell.

"I stole something once," Skeeter went on, still staring out at the ocean. "I was somewhere around your age. We were in this store, and I saw something I wanted. I guess I didn't have the money or something, or maybe I just wanted to see if I could get away with it. Anyway, I took this thing, whatever it was, I don't remember."

"Did you get caught?" Zach asked, his voice not much more than a whisper.

"Nah. But I lived in fear for about a year after that," Skeeter said with a little laugh. "I think I suffered worse than if I'd gotten caught and punished."

"Skeeter," Zach said in a low voice, "did Mom tell you about Zoey's piggy bank?"

"She mentioned something about it, yeah."

"She told you to talk some sense into me, didn't she?"

"You heard her, huh?" Skeeter said with a little smile. "You know what, amigo? She's worried about you, and so's your dad. Whether they're crazy or not, they love you and they care about you. Otherwise, they wouldn't be worried, right?"

"I guess," Zach mumbled.

"So what have they got to be worried about?" Skeeter asked.

Zach shrugged, sighing. "I don't know," he said. "I guess because the police brought me home that time we skated on the steps of the school, and Brian bumped into this lady, and her baby in the stroller almost went into the street."

Skeeter shook his head. "You've gotta be more careful than that, dude."

"I know, I know. It was just that stupid Brian," Zach said. "It's always Brian."

"Brian, huh? He's the ringleader?"

"Huh?"

"I mean, he does something, you all do it?"

"Kind of. Everybody laughs at all his sick jokes, and I got my hair bleached and my ear pierced because of him."

"Mmm . . ."

"Now I'm supposed to get tattooed," Zach confided.

"Tattooed? Get out of here!" Skeeter said, surprised. "You're not gonna do that, are you?"

"I don't know," Zach said. "If the other guys all do it, I guess I would. But I don't like needles, and they say it hurts a lot."

"It does," Skeeter told him. "Believe me, it does. But not as bad as getting one taken off."

"How do you know?" Zach asked him. "Did you have one taken off?"

"Uh-huh. Stupidest thing I ever did, getting that tattoo," Skeeter said, remembering. "Her name was Isabella. That's a long name, man, but no, I couldn't just get a red heart. I had to have the name, that's how crazy about this girl I was. Two months later we broke up, and how was I supposed to explain my tattoo to the next girl I went out with? I *had* to have it taken off!"

They shared a laugh at poor Skeeter's misfortune. "So don't be stupid. Anyway, nobody needs to go through that anymore."

"They don't?"

"Nah, not when there's henna."

"Henna? What's that?"

"It's a kind of natural plant dye that stains your skin for a few weeks. They've used it for thousands of years in North Africa and Arabia. It's great, because if you get tired of a tattoo, it's gone pretty soon. And if you like it, you can always draw it again. No needles, either — you just smear it on yourself. Or better yet, you get one of the artists out here on the boardwalk to do you."

Zach's eyes were wide with excitement. "Can I?" he asked.

"Sure, dude," Skeeter said with a grin. "We'll both do it. My treat."

"Awesome!" Zach enthused. "I'm gonna go back and show the guys my new tattoo, and they're gonna think I went through major pain!"

They laughed again, and slapped five. "Come on, let's go have some dinner," Skeeter said.

"Can we have sprout sandwiches again?" Zach asked hopefully. "They were excellent."

"I've got something better planned for you tonight," Skeeter said. "Macrobiotic South Indian curry. Très spicy."

"I don't know," Zach said, frowning.

"Just kidding, dude!" Skeeter said, breaking into a smile. "Let's go get some pizza, okay?"

"All right!"

After dinner Skeeter said, "It's time to go to work."

"Work?" Zach asked, getting up from the table and stuffing the last slice of delicious California pizza into his mouth. "Whmf wkk?"

"You'll see," Skeeter said, putting on his backpack and pushing off with his skateboard down the boardwalk. "Come on!"

Zach followed Skeeter for about half a mile, until Skeeter said, "Here's good," and did an instant walk-stop move that made Zach blink.

"How'd you do that?" he asked.

"You've never seen that one before? Here, let me

show you." Skeeter demonstrated how, by pointing the toe of your front foot, you could step off the board with your back foot and let it come up into your hand — going directly from skateboarding to walking in just one step. "Your friends are gonna love that trick. It takes about six tries to get it right, and then it's yours forever."

While Zach practiced his stylish new dismount, Skeeter took off his black feathered hat and put it on the pavement, top down. Then he reached into his backpack and pulled out a set of devil sticks. "I made these myself, out of a special composite material," he told Zach as he started to do tricks with the sticks, using the two he held in his hands to manipulate the third, larger stick.

Skeeter was amazing, Zach thought, as he watched his uncle do dazzling maneuvers, throwing the stick high into the air, catching it with the other two behind his back, all while "dancing" on his skateboard.

A crowd gathered in no time. As Skeeter continued the show, they started throwing bills and coins into the hat. They all applauded when Skeeter took his bow, but before the crowd dispersed, Skeeter made an announcement.

"Ladies and gentlemen, thank you so very much. Now I want to show you the marvelous musical instruments I've made with my very hands. They're for sale at ridiculously low prices, should you wish to negotiate a purchase."

So saying, he removed two flutes from his backpack, stuck them both in his mouth at once, and began playing them in beautiful harmony.

After a moment, and another round of applause, he took out a set of bells — "from old-fashioned telephones," he told the crowd — and played them, making a wonderful, eerie ringing sound. The crowd oooed and aaahed, and soon Skeeter had made several sales.

When a mother bought a flute for her little girl, Skeeter took the money she gave him, and fished out the change. But before giving it up, he folded one dollar into a peacock, and handed the amazing creature to the little girl.

"Wow — you've got mad skills!" Zach told him when it was all over, and Skeeter was putting his things away and counting his money.

"I had plenty of time while I was recovering from my fall to develop those skills," he said.

"So this is your job, then?" Zach said.

"It is for now," Skeeter said with a smile and a shrug.

"Mom always says you've never had a real job," Zach told him.

He saw the pain in Skeeter's eyes. "She also thinks you're a bad kid, you say."

"True," Zach said thoughtfully.

"She just wants something more from us," Skeeter said. "And actually, I agree with her."

"What?" Zach said, stunned. "You do?"

"Yeah, in a way. I mean, this is a fine life for a guy like me, who doesn't care about money or the things it can buy. But I couldn't have a family and live like I do. And let me tell you, Zach — it's good to have a family. It gets lonely for me sometimes."

They were silent for a few minutes as Skeeter finished packing up his performing gear. Then Zach said, "You think Mom's right about me, too?"

"She doesn't really think you're a bad kid," Skeeter assured him. "You've disappointed her, and that's how she's showing it, by saying stuff like that."

"Oh."

"But she said when I talked to her the other day that you'd been doing better lately — helping Zoey and all."

"Oh, yeah. I paid back what I owed her, plus I gave her free lessons, and her friend, too."

"Good man!"

"Yeah, I got really tortured for it, too, when the guys found out," Zach told him.

"Mmm, yeah, I guess that could happen. But you know what? You've gotta be the one the guys all follow. Then you don't have to worry about what they think, because they're all busy thinking how to be like you."

Zach laughed. "What if they don't follow me?"

Skeeter smiled. "Then they miss out," he said. "Come on — let's get you hennaed. Gotta make those other kids jealous."

"Okay, you can look now," the henna artist told Zach.

He looked, and he liked what he saw. The stain was reddish, instead of bluish like the needle tattooing. But the screaming eagle was vivid and well drawn, and the Asian lettering in bands above and below the eagle made him look and feel like a skateboarding ninja.

"That'll last you a month or more," Skeeter told him as they boarded home.

"And after that?"

"You've got to locate a place in Moorehead City that does it. Either a tattoo place, or a manicure place maybe."

"Cool. Can you teach me some more tricks before bed?" Zach begged.

"Not tonight, partner," Skeeter said. "There'll be time for that after the exhibition tomorrow."

Uncle Skeeter was an awesome skateboarder, but some of the professionals in the exhibition were totally unbelievable. One kid about Zach's age bounced around on his board like it was a pogo stick, balancing himself on the top truck. There was a trio of boarders who did tricks by hopping from one board to another. And some of the tricks that were done on the half pipe made the whole crowd gasp.

"That was fierce!" Zach told Skeeter when the

exhibition was over. "I want to learn to do all of that stuff!"

"Whoa, easy there, dude!" Skeeter said with a laugh. "You've got one more day out here. There's only so much new stuff you're gonna be able to learn."

"Well, what should I do, then?" Zach asked.

"Do you do any tricks already?"

"A few. I've got kind of a simple freestyle routine."

"Cool. Show me. In one day we can work on that, add a few quick touches, and make it a thing of beauty."

"All right!"

That's what they did for the rest of the afternoon. Skeeter showed Zach how to do multiple 360s by using the upper body to drive the turns. He taught him how to jump to goofy position and back while in full motion. Mostly, though, he helped Zach improve his "mental game."

"Skateboarding's a Zen sport," Skeeter explained. "That means you have to unite your mind, body, and spirit. By hooking into the cosmic flow, you go with the moment and let yourself be part of something bigger, something perfect."

Skeeter's eyes were closed as he said the words, and Zach knew that was how he approached everything: making musical instruments, saving sequoia seeds, fixing skateboards — everything.

Zach was feeling tired and sad as they rode the bus back to the airport on Monday morning. "I wish I could stay longer," he said.

"Me too, partner," Skeeter replied, putting an arm around Zach's shoulders. "But you've got enough to chew on for a while. Next time I see you, you'll be a Zen boarder, and we can work out some routines for the two of us."

"Yeah!"

"And listen, Zach —"

It was the first time Skeeter had called him Zach the whole weekend.

"If you give your mom and dad a reason to have confidence in you, they will. It might take some time — parents are a little slow to catch on sometimes — but I promise you, it'll happen."

12

"So how was it?" his mom asked as she greeted him at the airport. "Skeeter called to say he really enjoyed seeing you."

"He's the coolest guy," Zach told her. "Y'know, mom, he really does have jobs. They're just not in offices. Uncle Skeeter's a rebel, like me."

"Oh." His mother smiled, and her eyes went soft. Zach could tell she was thinking of her little brother. "So you're a rebel, too, huh? Well, Skeeter didn't turn out so bad, I guess. Still, I hope you won't go *that* far with it."

Zach smiled a secret smile as they drove back home. He couldn't see himself ever living like Skeeter, no. But he felt that he'd found a true friend for life — one who knew lots of cool stuff and would be happy to teach him.

"Your friend Benny called while you were gone," his dad said. "He was asking about your school project. Have you guys done any work on it at all?"

Zach thought for a moment, trying to decide whether to tell his father the truth. *Be trustworthy, and you'll earn their trust,* he heard Skeeter's voice inside his head.

"We need an idea," Zach confessed.

"An idea!" his father said. "You mean, you haven't even started yet?"

"We'll start tomorrow," Zach assured him. "We still have two weeks, almost."

"Two weeks?" his mom chimed in. "My goodness. You'd better find an idea fast!"

"You know," his father said, "if this was anything to do with skateboarding, he'd have had the project finished by now."

Suddenly an idea hit Zach smack in the forehead. "That's it!" he cried out at the top of his lungs.

His mother, startled, jammed on the brakes. "Zachary!" she gasped. "Don't do that!"

"Sorry, Mom," Zach said, settling back in his seat. "But I just thought of the perfect project."

✤　　✤　　✤

"A skateboard simulation? That is so boss!" Benny said when Zach laid it out for him on the phone.

"I knew you'd like the idea," Zach said happily.

"There's, er, only one problem," Benny hedged.

"Problem? What problem?"

"I don't know anything about skateboarding. You'll have to tell me exactly what to program."

"That's what I'm here for. Still, I want you to see the course I set up in the driveway."

"Sure. How about after school tomorrow?"

"Great. My skateboarding friends from Brighton are coming over, which is good. I want you to meet them."

"Is that really necessary?" Benny asked.

"Totally," Zach told him. "They'll have lots of good ideas. I'm telling you, man, this project is going all the way. We're taking the trophy, Jack."

"Ah, I just thought of another possible glitch."

"Uh-oh."

"Little one. Teeny-weeny one."

"What? What?"

"This project is supposed to have moving parts. What are our moving parts?"

"Hmmm . . ." Zach thought hard, trying to envision the course he would design. "Okay," he said, "first of all, there's a seesaw. You skateboard up it, then down."

"Okay, that's one moving part."

"And, of course, there's the skateboard."

"Two. We're getting there."

Zach scrunched up his face, trying to squeeze more ideas out of his brain. "And the rider moves. We're gonna have him hopping from one board to another."

"Cool! Do people really do that?"

"My uncle Skeeter does it."

"Wow!"

"Okay, and we should make it so kids can design their own elements, like a simple interface. . . ."

"Hey, you know what?" Benny said. "I think we're in business."

"Absolutely."

"But we've gotta have a name for it."

"I've got it," Zach said. "Try this on — Skeeter-Skate."

"Awesome," Benny said. "I love it."

"Hey, hey, hey!" Brian greeted Zach as the boys all skateboarded up to his driveway after school next day. "I did the dirty deed, yo!" He rolled up the left sleeve of his T-shirt to reveal his new tattoo. It had a skateboard, all right, but the word *ragin'* had been misspelled!

"'Raggin'?' Zach asked gently. "What's raggin'?"

"Ragin', man!" Brian insisted.

Zach shook his head, and watched as the pain and panic crept into his friend's eyes. "I'm afraid not."

Brian let out a little whimpering sound.

"I'm sure they can take it out and leave all the rest the same," Zach said, trying to reassure him. Then he looked around at the others. "Did any of you guys get the same one?" he asked.

The other kids looked down. "We, um, didn't get the money to do it yet," Kareem said lamely.

"Bunch of wusses, all of you," Brian growled, rolling down his T-shirt sleeve.

"The skateboard looks awesome, though," Zach offered.

"Thanks," Brian mumbled.

"I got tattooed, too," Zach said with a sly grin.

"Yeah?" Brian asked, brightening.

Zach nodded, and pushed up his T-shirt sleeve for them to see. All the guys aahed and oohed at the screaming eagle.

"Now that is phat," Sam said.

"And I didn't even have to get any needles." Zach told them about henna, and soon they were all excited, making plans for their temporary tattoos. They were all going to get eagles, to match Zach's.

That made Brian really furious. "Hey, what am I supposed to do with mine?" he asked.

Zach shrugged, and they all shrugged with him. "It's okay to be different, Brian," Zach told him.

"Shut up, Halper," Brian muttered.

Zach shrugged again. "Hey, guys, check out my skateboarding course!" He showed them the setup, and when they saw the cones and the ramp, they couldn't wait to try it out.

"Awesome!" Jerry said. "This is so cool!"

They all high-fived him and nodded appreciatively when he told them he owed it all to Zoey. "If I hadn't been giving her lessons, I would never have thought of it," he said.

Benny showed up then, and Zach introduced him. Benny shook hands with all the guys. Zach could see that he was feeling kind of awkward, so he stepped in. "Benny and I are designing a skateboard simulator for our computer engineering class," he said.

"You skateboard?" Brian asked Benny.

"Me? Uh, no."

"Wanna try?"

"Uh, no thanks. I don't think I could —"

"Aw, come on. Just once," Brian urged him.

Benny, looking caught in a trap, got on a skateboard, and no time was flat on his keister in the driveway. Brian howled with laughter, and the other kids, as usual, followed suit.

"Shut up, all of you!" Zach scolded them. "It's not funny, can't you see that?"

"I think it's a riot," Brian said, coming up to him and frowning.

"Anybody else think so?" Zach asked, turning to the others. He looked them in the eye one by one, and each of them slowly shook their heads no.

"Don't let him bully you!" Brian told the others. "Hey, check this out! I'm Fatty Flatfoot!" He danced around like he was Benny falling off a skateboard, and fell to the ground laughing. But none of the others even smiled.

"That's enough, Brian," Zach told him, standing over him in the driveway. "Benny's cool. He's a lot funnier than you are."

"Oh, yeah?"

"Any day." Zach turned away, leaving Brian lying on the ground with a stupid expression on his face. To the others, Zach said, "Now about our simulation. We were hoping you guys could give us some good ideas —"

"An A-plus!" his dad said, holding up the paper Zach and Benny had handed in with their project. "'Shows great creativity and effort. Congratulations!'" he read. "Well, well. I guess you're turning things around, son." He patted Zach on the back.

Zach nodded, but he was too busy right now to give his dad any attention. He and his friends were all planted in front of his computer, playing Skeeter-Skate as Zach and Benny proudly looked on, giving instructions.

"If you double-click, he jumps," Benny told Sam, who was in control of the mouse at the moment.

Sam made the rider jump, and the animated mosquito made a leap from one skateboard to the other.

"Yowza!" Sam said. "I did it! Man, I've gotta try that next spring, when they open up Moorehead Park again."

Snow had fallen that morning. It was only early November, but Moorehead City had long winters, and they'd be doing more snowboarding than skateboarding for the next few months. Still, it was great to be able to come inside and see skateboarding tricks.

The sound track Zach had added really made the visuals come alive, and the tricks the Brighton kids had helped come up with looked great on the screen.

It was going to be a fun winter, Zach thought, watching his old friends and his new friend laughing together. Zoey was there, too, with Lorena. She flashed Zach a big grin and came over to whisper in his ear.

"I can't wait to show those boys my tricks!"

Zach nodded, smiling. Zoey was going to show them a thing or two, all right. He'd made sure of that. He'd taught her well, just as Uncle Skeeter had taught him well.

Yes, things were definitely looking up — in fact, they were looking fantastic!

Matt Christopher

Terrell Davis	*Tara Lipinski*
John Elway	*Mark McGwire*
Julie Foudy	*Greg Maddux*
Wayne Gretzky	*Hakeem Olajuwon*
Ken Griffey Jr.	*Briana Scurry*
Mia Hamm	*Emmitt Smith*
Grant Hill	*Sammy Sosa*
Derek Jeter	*Mo Vaughn*
Randy Johnson	*Tiger Woods*
Michael Jordan	*Steve Young*
Lisa Leslie	

MATT CHRISTOPHER

The #1 Sports Writer for Kids

Read them all!

- Baseball Pals
- Baseball Turnaround
- The Basket Counts
- Catch That Pass!
- Catcher with a Glass Arm
- Center Court Sting
- Challenge at Second Base
- The Comeback Challenge
- The Counterfeit Tackle
- Crackerjack Halfback
- The Diamond Champs
- Dirt Bike Racer
- Dirt Bike Runaway
- Double Play at Short
- Face-Off
- Football Fugitive
- The Fox Steals Home
- The Great Quarterback Switch
- The Hockey Machine
- Ice Magic
- Johnny Long Legs
- The Kid Who Only Hit Homers
- Long-Arm Quarterback
- Long Shot for Paul
- Look Who's Playing First Base
- Miracle at the Plate
- Mountain Bike Mania
- No Arm in Left Field
- Olympic Dream
- Penalty Shot

Pressure Play

Prime-Time Pitcher

Red-Hot Hightops

The Reluctant Pitcher

Return of the Home Run Kid

Roller Hockey Radicals

Run, Billy, Run

Shoot for the Hoop

Shortstop from Tokyo

Skateboard Renegade

Skateboard Tough

Snowboard Maverick

Snowboard Showdown

Soccer Duel

Soccer Halfback

Soccer Scoop

Spike It!

The Submarine Pitch

Supercharged Infield

The Team That Couldn't Lose

Tennis Ace

Tight End

Too Hot to Handle

Top Wing

Touchdown for Tommy

Tough to Tackle

Wheel Wizards

Wingman on Ice

The Year Mom Won the Pennant

All available in paperback from Little, Brown and Company